The Makepeace Experiment

ABRAM TERTZ

The Makepeace Experiment

*translated from the Russian
and with an introduction by*
MANYA HARARI

NORTHWESTERN UNIVERSITY PRESS

EVANSTON, ILLINOIS

NORTHWESTERN UNIVERSITY PRESS PAPERBACK EDITION
Northwestern University Press, Evanston, Illinois 60201

Published in the United States of America

Translator's Note

The Makepeace Experiment is a novel and a fairy-tale as serious and as lighthearted as Orwell's Animal Farm. The story is based on the events in Russia over the past half-century. In order to uncover their roots in the nature of man and of politics, Tertz shifts their perspective, strips them of the myths which surround them and substitutes his own, with an abandon and detachment unequalled by any other Russian writer so far. Thus, if Lenny Makepeace is a composite portrait of several Soviet rulers, he is also a fictional hero in his own right, as well as the Dictator as such, who belongs to any country and to any age.

His name helps to explain his character and for this reason the translator has anglicised it, but in its original form, Lenya Tikhomirov, it carries more overtones than it does in English. Tikhomirov, made up of *tikhy* ('quiet') and *mir* ('peace' or 'world'), suggests both 'peace and

7

quiet' and 'world peace', while Lenya has connections with Lenin, with *len'* ('idleness') and with Leshy, the spirit of the woods in Russian folklore, referred to in the text as 'the wizard who rules over these parts'. A man of peace like Khrushchev, an illusionist like Stalin, a tormented rationalist like Lenin, Lenny is also a poor boy who believes that fate owes him a living and a peasant tsar endowed with magical properties by his people and inscrutable to the West.

Lenny is not the only author of his own fate. If, in the Marxist view, Communism is the apotheosis of history, prepared by its forerunners over the past millenia, Lenny's régime too is the result of a historical process: it is the outcome of the centuries old Russian dream of a 'mighty and benevolent Tsar' and of a century and a half of ferment among the intellectuals and the upper class.

The scene of Lenny's operations is Lyubimov, a small town which might well be the one within driving distance of Chekhov's Cherry Orchard where Grandpapa Gayev once doctored his serfs with sealing wax. Lenny's ancestor, Samson Samsonovich, was an equally strong personality and his spirit still broods over his native town. A nobleman brought up on Russian fairytales by Pushkin's nurse and married to a liberated serf, a scientist who corresponded with Lavoisier, a theosophist who went to India, a friend of Tolstoy and like him obsessed with the need to 'restore love to the human heart', he threatened Nicholas I at the time of the Decembrist rising in 1825 and has since had his finger in a number of experiments and 'miscalculations', the October Revolution among them.

Samson's direct heirs, like Gayev's, have emigrated to Paris, but among his obscure descendants is Lenny, a child of the new age, with a gift for gadgetry and a predisposition to politics—at least to the extend that he can be possessed by an idea and believes that 'man like everything else can be improved.' Once his ambition has been aroused by his passion for Serafima, Samson drops on him his mantle or, to be exact, his 'little book'—a manual of Oriental magic, which Lenny finds to be strangely consistent with the teaching of Engels and from which he learns the secret of success, 'magnetism'.

This is not of course a completely new revelation: it is the secret weapon of all dictators. Lenny merely develops to a unique degree the politician's gift of selling himself and his myth and of thus ruling by consent. He literally feeds the population on his dreams. They eat toothpaste and get drunk on water, convinced that they are feasting on caviar and champagne, and on this diet they dig ditches as enthusiastically as they did under Stalin and as then allow themselves to be dispossessed and their money to be turned into wallpaper for the élite. The difference is that all this is achieved without terror.

Of Stalin's two weapons, terror and propaganda, Lenny, like Khrushchev, genuinely prefers propaganda as kinder, cheaper and more effective. So much greater is his gift for it than either Stalin's or Khrushchev's that he is able to dispense with a police and an army. The Marxist utopia of the withering away of the State is thus achieved, and he looks forward to the day when all the nations shall be at peace, the city of Lyubimov (renamed Makepeace) their centre, and himself the lord of the world if not of the stars.

But Lenny goes further still; not only does he improve on Stalin and Khrushchev but also on Lenin and Engels. Lenin said that socialism (the new outlook) plus electrification (the scientific revolution) equals Communism (the happy future) and Lenny starts with the same assumption. But to a young man with a nervous but basically indolent disposition, living in a backward town, short-cuts are precious. If the outlook is sufficiently new, may not electrification, too, be dispensed with? Lenin only convinced the people that the future was already contained in the present for those who had the clairvoyance to see it, but Lenny convinces them that it is already there for all of them to touch, smell and taste: their consumer needs thus satisfied, what else can they want? His (or Samson's) is the crowning scientific discovery: not only can science produce an *ersatz* for almost everything but the scientist can produce an *ersatz* for science itself once he gets to work on the mind. Following and developing Engels's maxims that 'everything is flow and change' and that 'mind is the highest product of matter', Lenny shows that mind at its highest point of development produces mental matter—thus incidentally proving that man can live by mind alone.

Lenny's political success presupposes the temptation of all harassed men to lay down the 'burdensome freedom of everyday life' and give up their will 'if only to a monster'. This temptation is particularly strong for the citizens of Lyubimov, who live dreary lives, dream splendid dreams and are unsued to responsibility. Why then does he fail in the end?

One reason is that, as usual, Samson Samsonovich has miscalculated and is dissatisfied. He is even frightened. A nineteenth century humanist, however recklessly curious and experimental, he never meant to fly in the face of nature. Like Communism as seen by both its friends and its enemies, Lenny's régime has an apocalyptic air, though merely in the sense that man, relying on his intellect alone, is in danger of getting out of his depth and delivering the world to Satan. Samson Samsonovich doesn't like it.

Another reason is that the Russian attitude to the consumer paradise has always been ambivalent. Faced with the vision of it, Lenny's chronicler has the same reaction as the hero of

Mayakovsky's *Bedbug* when he awakens in a brave new world: 'better to hang by the tail from a eucalyptus branch' than exhaust the pleasures of a magical supermarket and be faced with a metaphysical void in the end.

There is also the resistance to hypnosis of the earth and of those who live close to it. The peasants (though happy to believe in spells as in miracles) are almost unsusceptible to the euphoria which Lenny is able to induce in the workers in town. A minimum of bread is needed, and, like other Soviet leaders, Lenny is defeated by the agricultural problem.

Finally there is the effect of dictatorship upon the dictator, and Lenny's inevitable human inadequacy to his daemonic role. The last day of his reign is as terrible as Stalin's. His failing power over others is temporarily restored to him but his own intentions escape his control and his kingdom reflects the chaos in his mind. Turned into warring devils and Gadarene swine by his random thoughts, his subjects take the task of their own destruction upon themselves.

Such is Lenny's tragic end as a ruler. But Samson finds peace for his soul with the help of another of his descendants, Lenny's mother, one of the innumerable Russian babushkas, as changeless as the trees, rivers and stones, and equally unaffected by the atheistic litanies she has been forced to mutter. It is perhaps on this submerged rock that Lenny the illusionist has ultimately foundered, but perhaps also thanks to it he survives, and Russia's history goes on— the city once again in the hands of the police, the old women praying for the living and the dead, and the doom of the world for the time being held off.

The Makepeace Experiment

Numbered footnotes are by the author,
who uses them as a literary device;
those with asterisks are the translator's

Prologue

~~~~~~

This is the story of Lyubimov, a city perhaps
more ancient than Moscow itself and which might
easily have become as important as Magnito-
gorsk*—all it needed was a railway and an oil-
well conveniently in the neighbourhood. But the
ways of progress have passed us by, and there is
nothing within miles of us but marsh, bog and
stunted woods in which the only game is hare and
a few varieties of inedible birds.

It is true that there is good shooting beyond
Wet Hill, a district famous for its wild duck
which are said to have been so plentiful in the old
days that they were exported by the cart-load
but regarded locally as scarcely fit for the pot.
But not even the oldest inhabitant has ever seen
bison or tapirs or giraffe. So Dr Linde's story of
coming across a prehistoric pterodactyl at the foot
of the Hill must be sheer invention. I did read of

*Main European centre of Russian metallurgy.

17

a single specimen surviving on some African lake but there are certainly none in our parts. What he must have come across (if anything) was a bittern. Bittern have a terrifying way of booming in the dark.

But the town itself is attractive and cheerful, the people are wide-awake, the Komsomol* has a lot of members and there is a fairly dense stratum of intellectuals. A couple of years ago— before the events—things were further livened up by the arrival of Serafima Petrovna Kozlova who came straight from Leningrad to teach a foreign language in our top forms. She at once became the main attraction at all picnics and charades and there was no one like her at a birthday party : one glass of champagne and she turned white and, with a yell, whirled away in a Caucasian dance, a naked knife-blade thrust between her teeth— all you could see was her elbows flying. She truly amazed us.

Yet she was much too proud for anyone to take any liberties with her. Dr Linde went nearly out of his mind. He had bet us two dozen bottles of beer: 'Give me two evenings,' he'd said, 'and I'll be on intimate terms with her.' Well, we drank his beer and laughed. The furthest he ever got with her was her fingertips: about a finger nail and a half. Just out of sportsmanship, I once tried an experiment with her myself. She had dropped in at the Town Library and

*Communist Youth League.

asked me in a bored voice for something to read.

'What about *Dear Friend* by Guy de Maupassant?' I suggested with a piercing glance. 'It's a very dissolute novel about French life.'

'No, thank you, I don't feel like it somehow.' She yawned and stretched, her breasts straining at her blouse. 'I'd sooner have something by Feuchtwanger or by Hemingway.'

That made me sit up.

'What d'you mean?' I asked in a whisper. 'We don't have any such things. We finished with all that rotten stuff in '47*. We got special orders from Moscow about Feuchtwanger.'

'Really? I didn't know. Then would you please give me *Spartacus* by Giovagnoli? I like an adventure story to read in bed.'

'That you can have. As many adventure stories as you like. We actually have two copies of *Spartacus* in our town . . .'

And all the time I was kicking myself! I was old enough to be her father. And I'd read her Feuchtwanger and her Hemingway (there's nothing so very special about them) and if I'd had one Serafima in my life I must have had fifty—some had even worn hats. And yet just because this chit of a girl came from Leningrad and had been to College, she could so embarrass me that I had to drop my eyes! What it is to be a provincial!

I forgot to mention our architectural monu-

*When cultural policy was tightened up after the war.

ments. We have a former monastery in our city, built in mediaeval times. After the Revolution the holy Fathers were sent to corrective labour in Solovki and in 1926 there turned up a Professor with a work party to do research and discover the secrets of the past.

They spent all that summer poking about in the ruins, measuring and digging—looking for a mummy, they said. But of course we knew better. Buried treasure was what they were after—gold, something solid to lay their hands on—but they never found it. All they dug up was a skeleton of a monk with boar's tusks instead of teeth, and with that they went away.

Many of us at the time were curious about those tusks and went to the lecture the Professor delivered gratis—about the formation of the earth from the sun and the origins of the animal and vegetable worlds. I too was sufficiently interested to drop in on him. I remember tying a silk sash over my Russian shirt, and putting on a straw hat, and strolling across to the dig. 'Good morning,' I said politely, raising my hat. 'And how is your research getting along?'

The Professor—he was in plimsoles and so modest, so unassuming, you would scarcely have known him for what he was—he gave me a friendly look and ran his frail, elderly hand over his small silvery beard. He had a wedding ring on, I noticed. 'Well, well,' I said to myself 'A representative of the Old Régime!' I took my hat off respectfully and fanned myself with it, smiling. Suddenly he took a step towards me:

'Perhaps you can tell me, young man.' (I was still in my twenties.) 'There used to be an ancient chapel hereabouts. Where was it exactly and where has it gone to? I can't understand it at all.'

And when I pointed to an empty space and told him all about it—how our chapel was blown up during the struggle against illiteracy, because it was the object of too much veneration and the centre of popular gatherings, mainly consisting of women, and because of certain coincidences, such as when a blind man miraculously recovered his sight; and of how there was not enough explosive, so that the work had to be finished by hand (they wanted the site for a bakery); and how afterwards the Chairman of the Town Council was burned to death on Christmas Day, and Maryamov's arm withered, and Pasechnik, who had egged everyone on, was hit on the head by a log at the sawmill (they carried him home and he died before the night was out)—when I told him all this, the Professor looked at me with an even warmer expression and said:

'You should write it all down in a notebook, in chronological order, young man. Your truthful chronicle of the life of your city would make a valuable contribution to the history of mankind. It would serve the common cause and perhaps make you as famous as Pushkin.'

Being young at the time, I didn't take him

literally. All I thought about in those days were girls, flirtations, teaching myself the guitar in twenty lessons, cycling . . . But the years went by and suddenly there I was—a widower with a bald patch on my head, my daughter Ninochka married and no longer the same love of cycling in my heart.

It was then I began to reflect. What's the point of all this agitation, I asked myself. Why should a man struggle and exert himself when he can pick up a book and on the very first page get himself a new wife and children, a new home and a mass of colourful impressions—all virtually without any risk? For the point of reading is, of course, that all the while your soul is drifting about the world—sailing the high seas, fighting with swords, suffering and ennobling itself—your body sits comfortably in an armchair and you can even quietly smoke a cigarette and enjoy a refreshing drink. You can forget everything, you can become Spartacus if you like, or King Richard the Lionhearted (out of Walter Scott), yet neither your absenteeism nor your political initiative runs you into the slightest danger. You put down the book and relax, and bask deliciously in your safety.

The only bitter moment is when you realise that the author has been letting his imagination rip. There you were, sweating and suffering with his heroes, cold shivers running up your spine, and it turns out that he made it all up! This I don't hold with. The writer should write about what he has seen for himself or at least learned from a reliable source; the reader should be given useful information to contribute to his mental development, and not made to feel he has been wasting his eyesight. What the reader wants, after all, is his pound of flesh and somebody's blood—you can't expect him to feed on air.

My own passion for literature developed after I was appointed Municipal Librarian. From reading to kill time, I became addicted to it. Then I tried my hand at writing. I wrote verse. It wasn't bad—even the rhymes. But I still felt that something was lacking, though I couldn't make out what it was. It was then I recalled my conversation with the visiting Professor in 1926. 'Ah!' I thought, 'if only something would happen in our city! If only there were a fire or a political trial! How gladly would I immortalise it for the generations to come!' It wasn't as if many people came to the Library. Apart from Dr Linde dropping in for a chat on the progress of science, or the Regional Inspector calling to see what the papers were doing about the shortage of cattle, there was only one other who came regularly—but I'm not saying anything about him yet . . . Yes, it was there, in the library, under my very eyes, that he met Serafima Petrovna Kozlova and it all began . . . But all in good time.

One day I came to work . . . No, that won't do.
One day I went out . . . No.

You wouldn't believe how difficult it is to begin, to put down that opening sentence which triggers off all the rest! Afterwards it gets easier. Afterwards, as I know well, it gets so easy, it goes with such a rush, that you can't turn the pages fast enough. You write and you can't imagine where the words are coming from—words you never meant to use, words you've never even heard in your life! —Yet they bob up of their own volition from under your pen and go sailing down the page, all in good order, like so many ducks or geese or black antipodean swans!

It gives you such a fright, you fling your pen away and say: 'It isn't possible! It can't be right! I can't have written that!' But you look again and you see that everything has been put down correctly, exactly as you saw it happen.

God almighty! What can it mean? I swear I'm not directly responsible. Is it possible that not only is our city under a spell, but I myself am regularly wound up and set in motion by some invisible hand?

I warn you, whoever you are: if I'm caught, I'll deny everything. If I have to stand my trial, hands and feet bound, face to face with a terrible judge, I'll recant, I'll say there's not a word of truth in it. —'Citizen Judge,' I'll say, 'I've been slandered and confused and tripped up. You can shoot me if you like but I'm an innocent man.'

Now I come to think of it, this may be the very reason why it's taking me such a time to begin.

That wretched first sentence may have been sitting in my addled brain all along and I just can't bring myself to put it down. —It's simply that I want to stay alive! Well, who wouldn't? It's nice . . . Nice to have a drink and a cigarette . . . Nice to read a book in peace and quiet (reading isn't like writing). Nice to go fishing . . . or have a steam bath . . . or an argument with Dr Linde about pterodactyls . . .

There it is again—pterodactyl! How could I possibly have thought of such a foreign word? I can't even pronounce it, and there are certainly no such creatures in our parts, as I've already said! I won't have it! Get out, whoever you are! Avaunt!

One day I went out into the porch and I saw. . .

Wait! Not so fast! First of all, why 'I'? Why this stupid habit of always putting oneself on the spot? Especially when it wasn't I, it was he who came out—Leonard Makepeace himself, our best mechanic and bicycle repairer in town! And secondly, all these details are a terrible nuisance. Once you talk about a porch, you have to describe it—was it low or high and were its pillars carved and if so . . . and so on and so forth . . . until very soon you are writing quite a different story.

To avoid this difficulty, chroniclers and historians make use of footnotes and I propose to follow their example. Thus if any reader wants to, he can take a breather and look up the details that interest him. But if he can't be bothered, let him by all means push on ahead as fast as he likes.

And now, let's begin.[1]

God, it's terrifying! It's just like being an inveterate drunkard—it pulls you, you can't help yourself, you feel the rush of irresponsible words to your head.

Well, let's get on with it.[2]

[1] It was the 1st May, 1958.
[2] Bless us, O Lord.

Chapter One

Coup d'Etat

―――――――――――――――――――――――――――――

One morning Leonard Makepeace, dressed in a
new steel-grey suit and with sandals on his bare
feet, came out and stood in the low porch of his
house. After a moment of indecision he drew a
small home-made notebook [1] from his pocket
and seemed to immerse himself in mathematical
calculations.

The weather was perfect. Clouds melted like
sugar lumps in the bright blue sky, everything
danced and shimmered in the brilliant sunshine
and Leonard, seen through the wattle fence,
appeared at a first glance to be wearing a golden
halo.

A closer look revealed that Makepeace could
not be merely doing simple sums in his notebook.
He was concentrating on it with all his might:
his lanky, narrow-chested body swayed in a

―――――――――――――――――――――――――――――

[1] Scribbled all over with minute writing.

curious rhythm, his breathing was laboured and two veins stood out on his forehead in the form of a V and were alarmingly swollen.[1]

Soon, however, the loudspeaker in the main square began to relay the musical overture to the May Day Parade and the sound brought Makepeace back to his surroundings. Snapping the notebook shut and putting it away, he uttered an enigmatic ' Ah! ' and relaxed.

'No, thank you,' he refused his mother's offer of a little cottage cheese and sour cream. (A frail old woman, shuffling in her felt slippers and clanking a pair of pails, she had joined him in the porch and was gazing at him devotedly.) 'You have some, Mama. I think I'll go for a stroll before breakfast.' He walked down the steps and vanished from the porch for the rest of the morning.

We will now look at the main square. It was echoing to martial music. A platform had been erected in the middle of it and upholstered in red cloth and upon this enormous crate the entire Administration stood, looking bright and alert and waiting for Comrade Tishchenko, Secretary of the Town Party Committee, to open the parade by ascending the tribune.

The whole square had been swept clean, the puddles filled with sand and not a single cow or

---

[1] Such swellings can cause haemorrhage of the brain.

sheep was nibbling the young grass. A red flag waved proudly in the wind from the top of the fire tower, while the five militiamen who formed the garrison were drawn up at the bottom, keeping a sharp look out for drunkards whose premature appearance in the square would have lowered the tone of the celebrations.

Clouds of dust rose gaily in the distance as the citizens advanced in procession from the far end of Volodarsky Avenue. Marching in the van were small children in white shirts, some waving flags or carrying paper lanterns, while others walked unburdened and unconcerned, guzzling sweets and smearing snot over their rosy cheeks. A few workers came next—men from the sawmill and employees from the food store and the post and telegraph office, followed by a couple of lorry loads of girls brought in from the collective farms.

Comrade Tishchenko watched the procession and as he saw the children—that sturdy younger generation marching to replace the old—tears of joy came into his eyes. His face as radiant as if he had breakfasted off buttered pancakes, he waved to the crowd, or held his hand to his peaked cap, or merely nodded, as much as to say 'Move on, citizens, we too would like a rest from our official duties,' while the citizens cheerfully scuffed up the dust in time to the music and shouted 'Hurrah! Glory to our valiant army!'

Suddenly there was a hold up. Instead of marching past, the crowd jostled in front of the tribune, looking up with curiosity at Comrade Tishchenko: he had raised his hand and opened his mouth as if about to speak but his face was working in perturbation and not a sound was coming from his lips, though even the loudspeaker had encouragingly lowered its voice.

We naturally thought at first that he wanted to make a statement on foreign affairs or to wish us a happy Day of Solidarity—not that it's usual to change the order of the proceedings and keep people out in the sun, listening to speeches, when it's long past their dinner time, but it was not for us to know who should make a speech on what, or why, if they had to, they couldn't get on with it. Ours was to listen to Comrade Tishchenko and drink afterwards. We weren't alcoholics, we could wait, it's never too late for a drink if you have the money. After Comrade Tishchenko's speech, there was nothing to stop us from drinking for the rest of the day.

But what Comrade Tishchenko had to say was totally unexpected. His voice strangled, the words coming a couple at a time with long pauses in between, he sounded as if someone were twisting his tongue and making him speak, while his mind was groping desperately in the dark, trying to make out what the devil had come over him.

'Dear fellow citizens!' He stopped in obvious

agitation. 'Dear fellow citizens . . . I wish . . .
We wish . . . to announce . . . that this day . . .'

He twitched, flushed crimson, and the next
words came in a rush, all on one note and in a
loud expressionless voice.

'This day marks the start of a new era in the
history of Lyubimov. I and the rest of the
leadership are voluntarily, I repeat voluntarily,
divesting ourselves of our functions, and I now
urge you unanimously to elect a leader to replace
us . . . a man who . . . our pride . . . our joy . .
I command . . . I beg . . .'

He faltered, gasped and, grabbing his neck with
his two hands, squeezed his windpipe as if trying
to stop the torrent of words. His eyes bulged,
his body swayed to and fro, the boards creaking
beneath its weight, and it looked as if at any
moment he would fall down dead, strangled by his
own hands, when a power evidently stronger than
his own loosened the deadly grip, freeing the
bruised throat, and his arms, still bent at the
elbows and looking like a crab's claws, were
slowly forced back. Standing in this defenceless
posture, he concluded:

'To elect as our supreme ruler, judge and commander in chief,'—his breath gasped and whistled
—'Comrade Leonard Makepeace, Hurrah!'

The silence was so deep that you could hear
the chattering of Comrade Maryamov's teeth.
As head of the special branch of the secret police,
he stood at his post on the edge of the tribune,

31

as pale as a one-armed statue.[1] The only other sound was the mooing of a cow in its untimely labour in some distant backyard.[2]

Within half a minute, however, isolated voices rang out in the crowd and very soon the whole multitude was stirring, rumbling and shouting its approval of the proposed resolution:

'Long live Makepeace! Long live our glorious Leonard!'

Only one village lout asked who Leonard Makepeace was and how he had deserved the highest of honours, but he was immediately shouted down:

'Don't you know our Lenny Makepeace? Our best mechanic and expert on bicycles! Disgraceful! Back to your village, you ignorant oaf!'

No one thought it strange that young Lenny, an obscure mechanic, should have suddenly been raised to such a height. On the contrary, everyone was astonished that his administrative gifts had remained unrecognised by our foolish bosses and that no leading position had been offered him until now.

'It's all Tishchenko's fault,' people were mut-

---

[1] This was the Maryamov who had lost his arm in the struggle against superstition.

[2] This was the cow which had been in the habit of infiltrating the square and nibbling the grass.

tering. 'He's the one who stood in our poor Lenny's way . . . Well, he's asked for it. Look at him now, paralysed—can't even straighten his arms—all humped up and twisted like an oven fork! Serve him right, the devil.'

The comments in the crowd were overheard by a swaddled infant of two months, asleep in its mother's arms—she had picked it up just as it was and brought it with her to watch the parade. Still too young to raise its head, it woke up, wriggled in its shawl, bared its toothless gums from ear to ear and squealed:

'I want Lenny to be our Tsar! I want Lenny Makepeace to be our Tsar!'

Its childish prattle was drowned in a thunder of applause. Mad with enthusiasm, the crowd clapped and roared, chanting the familiar syllables of the leader's name:

'Leo-nard Make-peace! Leo-nard Make-peace!'

There was nothing for it, Leonard had to step out of the ranks. Though still in his new, steel-grey suit[1], he looked bashful and a little embarrassed. In the middle of the square he stopped, bowed in the traditional manner to the four points of the compass and said:

'Sorry, comrades and friends, I simply couldn't think who you were calling for when I heard you shouting my name. I've done nothing to deserve such kindness. Still, if you wish it and

---

[1] It was for this occasion he had put it on.

33

insist on it I must reluctantly agree and bow to the people's will. I'll do my best to serve you— but one thing I beg of you: no personality cult! For the time being I think the Ministries of Justice and Home Affairs might as well stay in my hands. Of course the State is withering away, but we can't do quite without control, can we? What do you think, former Secretary Tishchenko?'

'Let go, Leonard,' Tishchenko moaned from his elevation. 'Let go,' he repeated menacingly, though unable to move a single joint.

Leonard only clenched his lean jaws, the veins swelling on his forehead and his expression conveying: 'If you think you're going anywhere, Semyon Tishchenko, you can think again.'

All the strength and authority seemed to drain from Tishchenko's body and suddenly—so the old women of Lyubimov say and such is the legend sprung from the imagination of the people —suddenly he spun round and toppled from the tribune like an idol overthrown. His head hit the ground and he vanished—but from where he hit it a feathered crow flew up with a loud squawk.

'Quick, a gun!' Leonard cried in a changed voice.

As usually happens, no one near him had a gun, but Makepeace was no fool; he took a run and threw himself face down on the same spot: immediately his arms developed the structure of wings, his legs contracted and folded up, and his grey suit turned into feathers. His beak stiffened and curved, his small, round eyes blinked, and a fully fledged hawk tore into the sky in pursuit of the screeching Tishchenko.

Swooping and diving like experienced pilots, they fought their air battle while, down below, the people marvelled and showed their approval of the new régime:

'At him, Lenny! Go for his eyes!'

But just as Lenny had forced him down and was about to sink his talons into the villain's heart, Comrade Tishchenko turned himself into a fox with a bushy tail. Had the rascal changed into a hare, our hawk would have made short work of him, but a sly fox is a match even for an eagle, so they say.

If you have ever seen a fox on the run you know that in the open country its evasive tactics make it quite impossible to catch it with your bare hands. But where was Tishchenko to hide in the city, with nothing around him but houses, fences, legs, girls hitching up their skirts to give Lenny a clear view? Heartened by the moral support of the population, Lenny changed his shape to that of a Borzoi. Dog though it is, this animal with its narrow face and long legs is as frisky as an antelope; its body is as involuted as a monogram and it leaps and weaves over the ground as if it were writing Chinese hieroglyphics in the air.

. . . he pounced, but the fox's brush was left in his teeth while the fox, without any loss of speed, proceeded on wheels as a riderless bicycle with mechanised pedals. People were still falling over each other, getting out of the way, when Lenny turned into a motorbicycle and chugged after the . . . riderless . . . mind the pavement . . . fox's brush . . . barking . . . up the hill! . . . go for his spokes . . . all feathers . . . mechanised, mechanised, Lord be with us! . . . a bicycle is no match . . .

But enough of this incident. It is as unfounded, as mythical as the legend of Elijah the Prophet, which in reality is an allegory on man's struggle with nature. The facts were very different. To discover them we must go back to where Tishchenko was imploring Lenny to release him from his bondage.

Almost all the strength had drained from his body when suddenly he seemed to experience a measure of relief and ordered the garrison:

'Arrest Comrade Makepeace—and we'll see who has the last laugh!'

His face came to life on his motionless torso and grimaced with spite.

A posse of militiamen creaking with ammunition belts marched up to Makepeace. Two of them drew their revolvers from their holsters and loudly and repeatedly discharged them at the loudspeaker. The music started again after the fourth round but stopped with a grunt after the sixth. The lawless régime of former Secretary Tishchenko had finally broken down.

The empty revolvers were dismantled and their component parts wrapped in a red handkerchief and handed to Makepeace. The disarming of the garrison was carried out in solemn silence and in battle order but with acrobatic skill. Leonard beckoned me over and entrusted me with the bundle.[1]

Meanwhile the garrison had collected flagstaffs and branches of fir trees and constructed a small portable platform suitable for a triumphal procession. Raised aloft on the broad shoulders of his stalwart guard, Makepeace looked like his own monument cast in bronze.

As he was being carried past the tribune where Tishchenko, still rooted to the spot, was now alone (the other former leaders having made off into hiding), Makepeace halted and said in a moralising tone:

'Take a good look! This shall be the fate of everyone who dares to encroach upon the freedom of our city!

'Long live the free city of Lyubimov!

---

[1] I had been standing in the crowd, about twenty paces away. When Makepeace crooked his finger and I ran up and took the bundle I felt a slight electric shock and heard an inner voice telling me to throw it into the river. This I did in the presence of Sergeant Mikhailov, who can bear witness to my unbalanced state of mind at the time.

'Long live technical and scientific progress throughout the world!

'Long live peace throughout the world!'

His eyes wandered, squinting more than usual, his hair was windblown and the dark V shone on his brow like a blood-red sign.

Two hours later the municipal telegraphist typed out the following message:

TO ALL. TO ALL. TO ALL.
THE CITY OF LYUBIMOV IS PROCLAIMED A FREE CITY. THE FREEDOM AND INDEPENDENCE OF ITS CITIZENS IS GUARANTEED BY LAW. WITHOUT THE SHEDDING OF A SINGLE DROP OF BLOOD SUPREME POWER HAS BEEN TRANSFERRED TO COMMANDER LEONARD MAKEPEACE. HEAR AND OBEY. SIGNED LEONARD MAKEPEACE.

Chapter Two, Which Explains the Events in Chapter One

—————————————————————————

To this day the discussion continues among the masses as to who Leonard Makepeace really was and by what mysterious power he succeeded in dominating the city. There are people who believe him to have been an envoy of God and others that he was sent by the Devil. Personally I stick to the view that there was nothing mysterious or supernatural about his origins and that his whole career can perfectly well be explained in scientific terms.

Leonard Makepeace came of a proletarian family. His father was a cobbler who fell in the war, shot down by a Fascist bullet. His mother was a simple and modest housewife, but one of her ancestors in the nineteenth century is said to have been a nobleman, Proferansov, who married a peasant girl after the liberation of the serfs. It is from him that Leonard is alleged to have inherited his passion for science and the talent for mechanical gadgetry which he showed from his earliest childhood. He once constructed a man-sized submarine out of old tins, which you could work by lying in it face down and turning its four propellers with your hands and feet. By a natural progression he became, at the age of seventeen, a mechanic in a bicycle repair shop. It was no more trouble to him to mend an inner tube, change a nipple or fix a slipped chain, than for you or me to drink a glass of beer.

The chief object of his research, however, was perpetual motion powered by the rotation of the earth, and he had sent a draft project by registered post to the Academy of Sciences in Moscow, but had so far had no reply. As usual, the bureaucrats stood in the way of progress. Little did they care about the obscure inventor's sleepless nights. Leonard endured his loss and disappointment with fortitude; his only fear was of the Americans stealing the project and using it to delay our victory.

'You are wasting your time, Lenny,' Dr Linde argued with him as they sat over their beer. 'Look at me. It's more than a year since I saw a prehistoric pterodactyl on Wet Hill and wrote an article about it and sent it to *The Medical Worker* but it's still lying about somewhere at their editorial office. Few people are moved by scientific discoveries. No one cares for anything but his pocket. The fact is that mankind is still at a very low stage of development.'

Dr Linde's moustache was ash-blond with beer foam and he claimed that it had a taste of salt. He licked it greedily, like a cat, darting his bright pink tongue at it, in the intervals of making pronouncements on various subjects with cynical paradoxicality. Thus he maintained that man is nothing but a monkey without a tail.

'You are wrong,' Lenny objected firmly. 'Human nature can be improved like everything else.'

With this he immersed himself in his thoughts, leaving the only glass he ever allowed himself unfinished as usual.

My own position was half way between the two extremes. I had even more experience of human nature than Dr Linde. On the other hand I liked Lenny's obstinacy, and I did not for a moment believe that progress had reached an impasse. I was firmly convinced that very soon we would invade the cosmos.[1]

I now believe that science will go very much further still and will end by lying in wait for us at every turn. The day will come when, just by pushing a button, any ordinary man like you or me will be able to satisfy his every need in a manner as yet undreamed of in our transitional epoch.

Imagine—you push a button and there and then, without your having to move from your

---

[1] History has since proved me right!

41

well-sprung sofa in your private room in a restaurant, there appears before you out of the thin air a table groaning with food and wine.[1] You eat your way through the menu, you stuff yourself till you are fit to burst, and you realise that the one thing you wanted all along and which is not on the table, the one thing which could have saved you from misery was a coconut, and you feel so lonely and so wounded and neglected that you could go and hang yourself. You push a button. A self-propelling trolley rolls in without human assistance, heaped with coconuts of every sort. But you don't want them any more, you say 'Take it away, it's too late,' and you push another button.

Immediately a trap door concealed in the parquet springs open and a golden-haired girl of ravishing beauty comes in answer to your summons. You push a button and all is well. You push it again and again, each time with the same result, but by now your heart is heavy and you say to her:

'Go back to where you came from, Lucy, I want to go on a long journey away from civilisation.'

One button takes you to Venice, another to Venezuela, a third to Venus or Mercury or perhaps to Pluto . . . And while the Devil is spinning you

---

[1] I imagine that spirits will still be rationed by the State.

round the universe you compose poems and songs in praise of the conquest of space, which are filtered into your brainpan by a special computer. And you make a face and say:

'Is this all there is? I'd be better off crawling with lice and rotting away in my primitive state, I wish I were swinging by the tail from a eucalyptus branch! Give me darkness! Give me shadow! Give me a patch of shadow to hide my face in shame!'

But how can there be shadow when light is pouring in from every side?

So you take to drink to drown your sorrows and as a sign of protest. You steal state-controlled vodka, you become a hooligan and a drug addict. You unscrew the buttons, you cut the cables with a knife, you put out the searchlights with a catapult.

If this tragic outcome is to be avoided human nature must be re-shaped. The old outlook must be forced out and a new one forced in. Once re-shaped, man will advance on the way to perfection of his own free will—he will even thank you for the benefits of science. This is what Leonard Makepeace understood and counted on. His intuition told him that bourgeois technology by itself would lead nowhere: it had to be backed up by a change of heart.[1] . . .

How can you say that? Didn't he change

---

[1] His intuition misinformed him.

everyone according to his taste? . . . and who are you anyway, putting words into my mouth?[1] . . . What makes you think you can order me about?[2] . . .

. . . Well, isn't that what I'm doing? So he said to her:

'I like you very much, Serafima Petrovna. Will you be my girl friend?'

'I can see you do,' she said with a quizzical look. 'But couldn't you be a bit more original?'

She smoothed her hair with an indolent gesture, raising her elbow to show her breast to better advantage, and Leonard, ablaze with passion, wrung his hands:

'I'll do anything for you, anything! I'll mend your wrist watch with my own hands and if you will allow me I'll arrange the doors of our future residence so that they open and shut of themselves at your mere approach . . .

'I'm a simple man,' he continued. 'I haven't been to college. But that doesn't mean I haven't got a scientific outlook, it's only that at present there's no institute in our town where I could qualify as an engineer. But despite the jeers of fate, I may yet distinguish myself and become famous; when my name is on everyone's lips then you'll be sorry. That day, I promise you,

---

[1] Stop philosophising and get on with the story.

[2] Get on with it or I'll push the button.

44

I'll plaster the walls of your bedroom with three-rouble notes—they'll look like green wallpaper—just for one kiss from you, and if I don't get it I'll go and hang myself.'

'What nonsense you do talk,' she put on a displeased expression. 'What's a kiss? Kisses are vulgar. And three-rouble notes are vulgar and cheap as well. You might at least make it hundred-rouble notes while you're about it. Mind you, I think money and riches are contemptible, but I do like a man to have ambition. "The madness of the brave is the wisdom of life", Maxim Gorky said. Only you'll have to think of something good if I am not to be ashamed of giving you my hand in friendship and of going through life at your side. Petty ambitions are no good to me. I don't agree with Julius Caesar who said it's better to be first in a village than last in a city—it's better to begin by being first in a city. So to start with, the city of Lyubimov will have to be at my feet, I mean at your and my feet jointly.'

She had completely changed her approach. There was an intriguing smile on her moist lips, an intoxicating promise in her eyes and a subtle hint in the tilt of her small, neat, appetising nose.

'I don't yet know what I'll do,' Leonard said glumly. 'No one as great as the men you speak of has ever come from our city. But I'll do my best.'

'Well, the day you come to me, borne on a shield and crowned with vine leaves like Spartacus, we'll get down to details. So long!' she broke off abruptly and vanished, sauntering out without even a hand-shake in farewell.

I was tactfully sitting behind a book case, reading *Novy Mir* (there was no one except the two of them in the reading room), but now I came out and spoke to Lenny as an older comrade:

'You listen to me, Lenny,' I said. 'You'd much better leave that tiresome woman alone. You've got plenty of talent but she'll suck you dry of every ounce of it. I know, I've seen plenty of them. You've got golden hands, Lenny, any girl would be glad to marry you—whereas in my opinion Serafima Petrovna is no longer a girl. Who knows, she may even have children of her own. And not only is she older than you, Lenny, but she's a Jewess, although she hides it, and that's something a Russian had much better steer clear of . . .'

'That's slander,' he spluttered, flying into a rage. 'It's sheer slander and prejudice. All nations are equal, and Serafima Petrovna has nothing Jewish about her, and her name is pure Russian—Kozlova comes from the Russian word *kozyol*, billygoat—whereas your name, Proferansov, does have a foreign sound and I'd like to know just how Russian you really are.'

'You're a fool,' I said, refusing to take offence. 'There have always been Proferansovs in our town, and if you really want to know, the sound is sheer music—Pro-fe-ran-sov—what could be

46

more harmonious? Not like your Chichikov, say, or Kukushkin! And another thing you should know is that your maternal grandmother was lucky enough to be a Proferansova herself, for she was descended from a certain learned philanthropist who later married a peasant girl and thanks to whom you also may have a little cultured blood in your veins. It's quite possible that you and I, Lenny, spring from the same root, only you have branched out into science and I into art.'

'What am I to do?' Lenny asked me despondently. 'You realise that for her sake I'm ready to commit murder. I'll just have to be a thief and a bandit—it's sink or swim for me now.'

'Why don't you read books instead?' I suggested. 'Look at all those shelves! Think—inside each of these bindings there is a great mind ready to share with you the fruits of his experience! A book is like a bottle of five-star brandy—you finish one and you want another. You could spend your whole life reading without ever getting bored, you wouldn't even know how the time had flown.'

From this moment Lenny became an inveterate reader. He had done some reading before, just to improve his general knowledge, but now you couldn't drag him away from it with a tractor. He gave up all his mechanical gadgets: all he did was to sit in a corner, moving his lips like a crazy hermit, and after a while he stopped even moving

47

his lips—only his eyes worked at a furious rate so that he could get through five hundred pages at a sitting (which, translated into another medium, is the equivalent of about half a litre). The books he borrowed at first were nearly always about great men such as Copernicus or Napoleon or Chapayev* or Don Quixote; he re-read *Spartacus* (a novel about Roman life) about four times. Then he became interested in the human brain and began to ask me for monographs on psychology and the nervous system and magnetic physics. I could see there was no hope for the man, his passion had unhinged him and he had gone to the opposite extreme so that not even Serafima Petrovna herself could do anything with him. She would come bursting into the library to change her adventure stories, but now Lenny didn't so much as show his nose from under the lampshade, and however much she pretended to be interested in what he was reading and hung over his shoulder, her breast missing him by half an inch, he paid no attention whatsoever to her antics. I sat squirming behind my desk, signalling to him as much as to say 'What are you waiting for?' But it was no good: there he sat, stuck in his chair as if he were nailed to it, his eyes running about on the page and not even seeing her. It made me blush for him when I thought of his ardent confessions to her such a

* Guerilla leader during the Civil War and hero of a Soviet novel.

short while ago, and that he had given up such a woman in exchange for nothing but dry books.

'Pity I ever warned him about her nationality,' I thought. Yet I had only done it for his good, because I know the toughness there is in that Jewish race which is scattered over the face of the earth like raisins in a pudding or pepper in a stew —but not like salt, because salt dissolves whereas the Jews keep their original properties, the ones God endowed them with. And perhaps the reason He has scattered them throughout the world is for them to show their toughness and enduring obstinacy, and for us—when we come upon them in the middle of our Russian stew— to remember that history didn't begin today and that no one can tell how it will end.

I once had a Jewess in my life—I won't forget her to my dying day. Black hair, all in wicked little curls, black eyebrows like two hairy caterpillars and a yellowish skin rather like Morocco leather to the touch . . . She spoke Russian like a Russian—you couldn't tell the difference—and the only Jewish word she knew was *tsores*, which in their language means sorrow or trouble, or a kind of prickly sadness littering the heart. There was a grain of this *tsores* buried in her like a raisin you could never dig out—immured in her as it were, mixed into the very composition of her soul. Even when she was laughing and tender her eyes were sad and there was something in them of the desert of Arabia, or perhaps the Sahara—the one

49

they crossed when they fled with their children and their belongings, and brought all the sorrows of the world along with them, laden on their backs and on their camels which also had drooping eyelids and Jewish expressions.

'Why are you sad, darling?' I used to ask her.

'I'm not,' she said. 'Why should I be? I know you'll end by paying me my twenty-five roubles and the ten you owe me for last week.'

She was being truthful according to her lights, for she was quite unaware that, from under her black eye-lashes and her camel eyelids, the parched desert was looking out, glazed with loneliness, and waiting for something, and drawing you somewhere, so that there was nothing left for you except to sit down on the sand and weep inconsolably over historical memories.

You can always tell a Jew by that desert expression in his eyes. I had seen it flashing on and off in Serafima's face, and the reason I told Lenny was to prevent his being burned up by it like the grass of the field and withering before his time. But now Lenny had other things on his mind.

One day I came back after lunch, as usual, and found Leonard in his place with a book and a pencil in his hand. He was sweating his guts out over the *Dialectics of Nature* by Friedrich Engels but what caught my attention was another book —one I didn't know—lying a little to the left of the *Dialectics*. It was an average-sized book in a leather binding so thick that if you soled your shoes with it you'd never wear them out in a century. I asked him what it was and where it came from.

'It fell on me from the ceiling last Friday,' he said, covering it with his hand. 'Luckily not on my head.'

He told me that the previous Friday he had been at home fixing the sink which had come away from the wall, and that they had a lot of rubbish piled up on top of their ceiling—they left it there to keep out the draught, layers and layers of it—worn-out shoes and coats and cracked pots and broken horse-collars and so on. Well, the plaster must have been as rotten as the rubbish and the book fell out as a result. After digging about in her memory, which was equally full of ancient rubbish, his mother told him it must have belonged to his grandfather, or perhaps to his father, a hereditary proletarian who had taken part in the Civil War when the nests of the nobility were being sacked and the serpents' brood strangled at birth.

'You know,' I said after thinking it over, 'it may very well have belonged to Proferansov himself, the nobleman I was telling you about, who lived in the nineteenth century and went in for scientific experiments and is even said to have squandered a fortune on an expedition to India.'

One word leading to another, he finally admitted that the book was a translation from the

Indian, transcribed in an elegant hand and entitled *The Magnet of the Soul,* and that it told you how to influence people and make a success of your life by using a mental force which is called magnetism.

'You be careful, Lenny,' I said, worried by the foreign sound of the word. 'Mind you don't yourself get influenced by some alien ideology. Are you sure it isn't a book on magic, which is contrary to the laws of nature and of scientific progress?'

But he quickly reassured me by quoting Friedrich Engels's *Dialectics of Nature.* He said it contained various propositions in support of the Indian theory, among others that mind is the highest product of matter, and that everything in life is flow and change, which could only mean that the mind itself can also change and produce a material result.

'That's very true,' I agreed. 'All the same it won't do any harm to throw that little book into the stove before anyone gets it into his head to report it. We can keep the binding and use it for shoe leather, it's of Tsarist manufacture, so it won't wear out.'

I put out my hand to feel the leather but the second I touched it an electric shock as strong as a blow in the chest flung me back into the middle of the room.

'You might have warned me.' I was shaking all over and seriously annoyed. 'How was I to know it was charged with electricity?' But Lenny was laughing like a drain.

'It's not the book, it's me, Savely Kuzmich. I'm charged with willpower. And now I'm going to make an experiment on you.'

Suddenly the room turned upside-down and I found myself standing on my head, keys, coins and matches clattering out of my pockets and the hem of my coat getting into my mouth. The oddest thing about it was that I felt no pain or discomfort, no rush of blood to the head and not even any nervousness about my blood pressure. I might have been a champion athlete and spent my life standing on my head! There was nothing wrong with my mind, I remembered everything and had all my wits about me, and I admired Lenny who could turn a man upside-down as easily as that. My arms felt unusually strong and springy, and I pranced on my hands and told him what a splendid fellow he was. I also said he needn't go on urging Serafima Petrovna to marry him because she would now surrender unconditionally, and that he could probably get a rise in pay from his boss at the workshop.

'That's small beer,' Leonard objected, launching into his favourite theory that a man's duty is to look after mankind:

'Work it out for yourself, Savely Kuzmich. Why are we so badly off, or rather, less well off than we might be? It's because no one thinks of anything but his pocket, it's because our

53

splendid country is still plagued by bureaucrats, routineers, hypocrites, thieves, teddy-boys, womanisers and decadents. Well, from now on we won't even have to put them in jail to straighten them out and to turn our motherland into a paradise. I'll simply imbue them with the right spirit and teach them the dignity of labour and the love of their country and show them how to improve its material and cultural standards *ad infinitum.*'

I stood on my head in front of him and grunted with pleasure. It was an intoxicating experience. He seemed to be enormously tall, stretching back and up towards the right hand corner of the ceiling. Only one thing puzzled me a little: why did he take the absurd risk of balancing on his two feet when it was so much easier, safer and more pleasant to stand on your hands? He must have his reasons, I told myself. It's for our sake, for the sake of the common man, that he's risking his life. He has to hold his head high so that he can see farther . . . Yet there must still have been a doubt left in my mind, or perhaps his hypnotic apparatus wasn't yet functioning perfectly, because I took one hand off the floor and by habit shook my finger at him warningly:

'You look out, Lenny. Mind your magnetic book doesn't mislead you into idealism.'

'Of course not, Savely Kuzmich,' he cried excitedly. 'I came to these conclusions long before I read the book. They have a strictly scientific basis. All I need now is a pocket magnifier to project my will and thought waves to a greater distance.'

He then explained to me the reciprocal action of energy waves and how every particle throughout the universe had its own rhythmic vibration, as illustrated by the rotation of the earth and of the two halves of the brain. This, he said, had already been noted by Darwin, Jules Verne and Count Cagliostro. All you had to do was find the common denominator of all these vibrations, bunch up your will and learn to project it on a single wave length. I don't remember all the technical details, but his illustrations were most convincing.

Finally he put the book away in an old brief case and said:

'Now, Savely Kuzmich, please resume your normal posture and pick up the things you dropped from your pockets.'

I stood up without much difficulty, though I felt a little dizzy, and hastily collected my keys, matches and coins.

'And now, old chap, forget everything you have seen and heard. I don't want you to give away my secret before the time is ripe.'

. . . and I forgot. I forgot about the book and about standing on my head. It was only two months later that the main outlines of the scene I have just described began to come back to me. I may not remember it all even now—how can

I know? How can I check up? At the time it seemed to me I was just back from lunch . . . I did wonder a little why my hands should be so dirty and so painful, and my coat crumpled, and why I should be feeling giddy and weak in the stomach, but my mind was completely clear and I remember thinking I must be getting too old for my job.

I went up to Leonard and saw that he too was a bit under the weather, looking green and mopping his face. He must have been overdoing it, I thought.

'What are you reading now?' I asked him.

'As you see, Friedrich Engels's *Dialectics of Nature.*'

'And what does Engels say in his *Dialectics*?'

'That everything in life is flow and change, and that mind is the highest product of matter . . .'

'He's quite right,' I said. 'That's very good about mind being . . .'

. . . I flopped down in a dead faint. When I came to myself, Leonard was bending over me with a worried look. He had filled his mouth with water and was sprinkling my face. He really cared for people, our Lenny, he really felt concerned.[1] He understood . . .[2] Damn, there's that voice again from under the ground . . .[3]

---

[1] I see no sign of it.
[2] Nothing.
[3] Or perhaps from the ceiling?

Or from the ceiling—how do I know where you've hidden yourself this time? . . .[4] What did you say? I can't hear you. Speak louder.

'I was saying that you and I are old friends, Savely Kuzmich.'

'What are you talking about? I can't see you. All I can see is that my pen is scribbling nonsense . . .'

'Don't you remember our talk at the excavation site? Surely you remember the Professor?'

'Are you the Professor?'

'Yes.'

'Good gracious, Professor! How are you? I never recognised you . . . Of course it's a good many years . . . Just a minute, that was in 1926 and you were an old gentleman then . . . Shouldn't you be dead by rights, if you'll excuse my saying so? I mean, isn't it rather strange?'

'Many things are strange, my dear sir.'

'Lord save us! Queen of Heaven, have mercy! . . .' All the while my accursed pen was writing on and on, clamped to my fingers. 'Excuse me, Professor, you don't happen to have a tail by any chance?'

'No. Why should I?'

'How should I know why . . . I was just wondering . . . And no horns?'

'No, no. I assure you—you are mistaken.'

'How am I to address you then?'

[4] · · · · · · · · · · · · · ·

'Go on calling me Professor. It's no good complicating the story with extraneous names and facts. We've digressed enough as it is.'[1]

'Will you at least do one thing for me, Professor? Will you show yourself just for a minute? Let me see you, recognise you, be sure it's you . . . After all we must meet some time . . .'

'That would be superfluous.'

'Are you looking at me?'

'I don't need to. I just use you to write with.'

'You what! And what am I supposed to be doing?'

'Really, Savely Kuzmich, you are impossible . . . All right then . . . we are writing the book jointly, in layers . . .'

'In layers?'

'That's right. If you want to explain the intricacies of Russian history, you have to write in layers. You remember the excavations at the monastery—how the various strata were uncovered in their chronological order?—eighteenth century shoe soles, sixteenth century shards and so on? Well, it's the same with writing. You obviously can't keep on always excavating at the same level. You've found it so yourself—look at all those footnotes and digressions, all these vaults and cellars you dig to make storage space for your facts. I only want to help you, and I'm

---

[1] At these words I felt the pen tugging at my fingers but I managed to hold it back.

willing to take on some of the descriptive passages myself. You will do the actual writing of course, but the ideas flowing through your mind will come from another source. Now don't argue, I've already had to guide and correct you several times—you would only have got muddled and fetched up goodness knows where. Take your Makepeace, how have you presented him? Anyone might think he was a sage or a magician, when in fact he was never more than an executive —a talented one, I admit, but still only an executive. You don't imagine it was by his own authority he subdued the city?'

'Of course. Who else's?'

'Mine.'

'That I won't believe! It's too much! I'm not even so sure that you exist! For all I know, I may be suffering from schizophrenia—it wouldn't be surprising after all I've been through—perhaps there's no professor, perhaps there's no one else here at all, I'm only talking to myself. Who do you think you are anyway? The idea of your giving orders to Lenny Makepeace, to our Russian Hercules!'

'Why orders? Why not a credit? We all draw on capital accumulated by our seniors. You for instance are at this moment writing with my help, in many ways individually, but all the same with my assistance.'

'I don't want your help! I can do without it! I'll simply hang on to my pen a bit tighter and

I'll do-oo it myself cell safe son some Samson Samsonovich let go of which how much five to twelve said the duchess and the plane with a menacing roar rose from the wood the woo the woodbine . . .'

'That's enough, Savely Kuzmich, it's not good for you at your age. You see what it is to be too self confident. So don't let's quarrel, we mustn't repeat the Makepeace experiment . . . It's absurd, in your position and when the city is almost . . .'

'And who are you to be criticising everyone else? Are you an angel or something? Are you God Almighty?'

'Come, come . . . You are too excited, you don't know what you are saying . . . It's just that I'm sorry for the city, I'm fond of it. There I spent . . .'

'One summer, Professor, one summer.'

'Not only. I was there before . . .'

'I don't seem to remember . . .'

'You, my dear sir, were not yet born. But why should we talk in riddles? My name is Proferansov.'

'This is beyond everything! Proferansov is *my* name. Didn't I tell you I was talking to myself! The cheek of it! Am I to have nothing left? No city, no Makepeace, I'm not even writing my book except under dictation . . . At least my surname is mine and I'm not giving it up . . . There's only one Proferansov in this town, I'm

the only one . . . Wait, I'm sorry, I forgot . . .
Are you *that* Proferansov?'

'That very one. Samson Samsonovich, at your
service.'

Before the pen dropped from my limp fingers
I heard, somewhere in the upper air, a brief
explosion of dry laughter and wrote:

'Hee-hee!'

Chapter Three

V-Day

I approached the city early at dawn, before the sun had risen over the wall of the monastery. It was the hour when the earth was still wrapped in an airy grey coating of mist, or rather, when each thing exudes the last of the nocturnal warmth and luminousness which envelop its bare dark bones as in a fleecy cocoon. Houses and fences look twice their size, a fleecy air current steals over the fields, and everything is large and kindly as in a fairy tale, and stirs and spreads and unravels before your eyes, as if it had nothing to keep it in order.

It was the hour when human beings are fast asleep, for as objects lose their substance in the world outside, they gain it in dreams. Flat out on their back or belly, bare feet sticking out, the sleepers are as quiet as the dead. But their meekness is deceptive. Inside the bony shelter to which they prudently withdrew the night before, the party was in full swing—crowds jostling, passions seething, glasses clinking and an anaemic proletarian astride the Governor's daughter, celebrating world revolution for the umpteenth time.

He shivers, pants, twitches his lips, chewing a dream cake. To look at his tense, livid face, the veins knotted on his consumptive brow, you'd think, at any moment he would start up from his damp couch and stride unseeingly into the street. But he won't budge—any more than the rest of the bare-footed corpses suckled by dreams. See how pale, how bloodless are their bodies! All their blood has rushed inwards, to where the rumpus is at its height—wakes and weddings are held, cannons fire salvoes and, at the merest indication of his wish, the Governor's daughter hurries in with a porcelain pot for the guest of honour.

. . . Hurry, hurry, enjoy your dreams! Your time is short. Already the roofs in former Nobility Street glitter with a metallic sheen, the guns of the *Aurora** have fired their first salute and brave red banners wave over the monastery walls. In less than an hour you will awaken, ragged, destitute, and rub your eyes, wondering where all the splendour has gone to—all the dreams and legends of Lyubimov, a city which even in its proudest moments never ranked

* The mutiny on the *Aurora* marked the outbreak of the Revolution.

as a provincial capital with a Governor of its own.

Never more than an obscure market town, lost amid its gulleys, bogs and woods, had it so much as kept its ancient name on the map? Or had it been carved up, reshaped and renamed after some wretched fellow who had jumped out of the bog and set off across Russia in his bark shoes never to be seen in his collective village again but to earn the rank of Major-General and leave his bones under Budapest?

No, no one from Lyubimov had as yet jumped to fame. And perhaps it was because of this that its early morning dreams were so fantastic and so full of envy. Just because other people had invented watches and machine-guns and opened a window on Europe, was it to be for ever satisfied? Was Lyubimov played out, sunk in its inertia to the end of time? Had it no ambitions, no tricks up its sleeve, no wish to astonish the world by a brand-new Utopia of its own? You'd soon see if you fattened it up a little and gave it its head, and a plan and a signal, and put the right man in the right place! Seriously, though, what would it do? What would happen if you said to it:

'Wake up! Your day of glory has arrived. Here you are, you have the chance to turn your dreams into reality. You can have your mighty and benevolent tsar. I give you a leader endowed with that intangible power you've been raving about for three centuries!'

No one arose, no one responded to the call which burst from my lips as I looked at the dishevelled little houses uncomfortably huddled in the hollow at my feet, and as I conceived my plan, so sudden and so daring that my blood ran cold.

They slept, unaware of the impending change. Only their breathing quickened and grew stronger, sweat beaded their temples and their faces crimsoned. The air whistled, hissed and roared through the apertures of their mouths, as if engines were at work pumping the blood from its vast nocturnal reservoirs to the opaque, smooth surface of the day. The reflections were brighter than the originals. As the colours vanished below, they were kindled with a tenfold intensity above. Dreams paled and weakened, lost their dignity and melted in confusion like a girl in a stranger's arms, while cheeks, necks, heels flushed, and the mounds and ledges of pillows and chests of drawers hardened and stood out, until finally the whole city bounced out of its bedclothes and went into action, preening itself on its pot-bellied samovars, its juicy window plants and the angry screech and clatter of carts in its cobbled streets.

A youth with a wasted brow leaned out of his window, smiled at his absurd thoughts and muttered in a soft, brittle voice, as if unsure of being awake:

'Good morning, my Lyubimov, my love!'

It was not until two days after the *coup d'état* that the news of the catastrophe reached the town of X.[1] It was brought by a one-armed refugee who arrived at dawn and awakened the Lieutenant of the guard. The Lieutenant, though half-asleep and chilled to the bone, immediately—on his own initiative and responsibility—rang up Lieutenant Colonel Almazov at his flat and reported in the appropriate low but clear whisper:

'B8/O speaking. Bear mating has begun in Lyubimov.'

'What? Whose mating?' shouted the Lieutenant Colonel, half-awake and forgetting the top-secret code he had himself introduced.[2]

'Bear twitters in Lithuanian. Time to slit its throat. Drowned corpse arrived by sledge, injection required . . .' continued the dispassionate voice with its undertones of tragedy. At last Almazov took it in.

'Detain the corpse. I'll be over at once.

---

[1] The regional centre 50 miles from Lyubimov, situated at the junction of the X highway and the X railway.

[2] Besides, it was confusing! the bird-mating season was on.

Where's my diving kit, Sophie? Sorry, chérie, I mean my revolver.'

Still covered with dust and exhausted by his journey, Maryamov, who had witnessed the lunatic events in Lyubimov, was questioned secretly, within four oak-panelled walls, by a joint board consisting of Comrades O and U and Colonel Almazov. His evidence made no sense. A revolt had broken out but the rebels had adopted peaceful and law abiding methods. An adventurer was at the head but the city had been handed over to him by the Secretary, 'Ironsides' Tishchenko himself. Lyubimov had proclaimed itself an autonomous region—something between a feudal Russian princedom and a Duchy of Luxembourg—yet its one desire was quickly to attain the common goal which the whole country was killing itself to achieve.

'Were none of the speeches political? Was nothing said about flour or sausage?' Almazov pressed the ingenuous witness.

Maryamov looked vague.

'Not that I heard of . . . What Makepeace seems chiefly to worry about is contributing to world progress . . .'

'Well, well,' said Comrade O (in an embroidered shirt, bald and with smiling eyes; even Almazov was a little afraid of him). 'Well, well! Sounds as if the riff raff of Lyubimov ought to be written up in the papers and the ringleader decorated! Yet here I have a manifesto telegraphed by an enemy agency—and incidentally delivered to me twenty-four hours late because our Lieutenant Colonel was too busy to bother with such a trifle! Of course it's a holiday—and then there's fishing and shooting—I appreciate all that even though I wasn't taught a foreign language as a child!'[1]

He unfolded the telegram, dusty with lying about at the post office and read out:

'TO ALL. TO ALL. TO ALL.'

His bald scalp rippled like sea waves, the wrinkles racing from the bridge of his nose to the top of his head where they formed thick folds like fleshy lips.

'What does "all" mean? It means that they address their loving message to *every* capitalist and landowner, *every* prince and baron who has cunningly escaped destruction, *every* champion of the Cold War, including the Pope of Rome who is only waiting to slake his thirst with the

---

[1] '*Diable!*' thought Almazov, taking in the oblique reference to his noble origin and his familiarity with French. 'So the bald tortoise has beaten me to it again—just when I thought I had him cold over Tishchenko! "Tishchenko, Comrade O's protégé, hands over the keys of the city!" Makepeace, Tishchenko, Comrade O— Oh, what a conspiratorial chain! What a shooting party, complete with decoy ducks, it would have started in the good old days!'

blood of the working class . . . But let's continue. "The freedom of the citizens is guaranteed by law." What freedom? Who is to be free and why? Who wants freedom in a free country? What they mean is "freedom" to sell their motherland, "freedom" to trade wholesale and retail in human beings as they did in the days of serfdom, "freedom" to close hospitals and schools and re-open churches at the behest of the Vatican, "freedom" to burn scientists at the stake as they burned Giordano Bruno . . . But we won't let them, Citizen Maryamov. We won't let them! This time they are going too far!'[1]

The deeper he went into the secret aims of the conspiracy, the more excited Comrade O became. He would often fumble at the beginning of a speech as he tried to call to mind the words of the latest hand-out on foreign affairs, but as soon as the resounding phrases left his lips, there was no more holding him and he sometimes worked himself up to such a pitch that he screamed, stamped and banged the table with his fists without knowing why. 'Eloquence, that's my trouble,' he complained when the attack was over. 'The minute I get started on the Vatican

---

[1] 'Old Maryamov will have to get a Strict Reprimand for Lack of Revolutionary Vigilance,' thought Almazov. 'Oh well, he should have kept his ear to the ground. *A la guerre comme à la guerre!*'

or the struggle for peace, I see red, I could tear them all to pieces with my own hands.'

His colleagues knew the signs and patiently hung their heads. Even Comrade U, who nodded in agreement at the end of every sentence, avoided looking up at Comrade O. No one had the courage to watch him—not because his expression was ferocious—on the contrary, it still kept the traces of his innate good nature and of the childish, inoffensive smugness of the man of humble origin, grown fat in office. But gradually, as he spoke, his face crawled up his head, the eyebrows twitching at the top and driven further and further back by the seething folds of skin: any moment, it seemed, the last link between bone and flesh would snap and a creased and bleeding lump of tissue drop at his subordinates' feet. They waited for this in terror, as if their fate hung by a thread—as if, at the very next twitch, everything would go up in smoke.

As usual, tragedy was averted—this time by Maryamov who had been sitting glumly in his corner while the telegram was being read and his own report on Makepeace analysed and denounced as absurd.

Unwashed, unshaved and in rags (he had spent half a day hiding in the bog and then run forty miles without a break before getting a lift from a lorry), the wretched witness of the *coup d'état* suddenly gave tongue:

'He's not going to re-open the churches,' he

muttered, taking advantage of an oratorical pause. 'You know best about capitalism and freedom, but you needn't worry about the Christian faith. It won't be Lenny who restores religion. I can tell you that!'

'Why not? What's this rubbish?' Astonished that a minor official should dare to heckle him, Comrade O was, in his heart of hearts, pleased at the interruption which gave him a chance to put his features back into place; he was already regretting his attack of eloquence which, he knew, was bad for his blood pressure.

'He just won't.' Maryamov stared at his feet.

'Well, go on, don't be frightened.' Something of his normal expression of benign amusement flashed in his eyes and Almazov and Comrade U looked up, relieved. 'Are you telling us that your Lenny doesn't care for God?'

'Come on, don't be nervous,' Comrade U seconded. 'Why doesn't your Lenny care for God?'

Maryamov rose, took a stumbling step forward, recovered his balance and squared his shoulders. They all realised how old he looked, how exhausted and how one-armed.

'Because Lenny Makepeace is a sorcerer! Because he's Antichrist! He has devils to assist him!'

Raising his one arm, he made a wide and fervent sign of the cross.

'Put him in solitary,' Almazov told the Lieutenant of the guard after Maryamov had been removed. 'No visitors until further orders. The old man is off his rocker. He'll get over it.'

To efface the unfortunate effect on his distinguished guests, he added:

'According to his dossier, Maryamov lost his arm as a young man, in the course of his anti-religious work. His break-down may well be the delayed result of this traumatic experience. Pity! Nerves, you know! They're the scourge of our profession. Ours is a risky game!'

He delicately stroked the silver strand in his dark, velvety hair, which went becomingly with his musketeer moustache. Fortunately Comrade O didn't notice, but Comrade U, whose hair was by nature as luxuriant as Almazov's and who might have been as successful with the ladies of X if he hadn't shaved it off out of loyalty to O, sighed and looked away.

'Well, well,' Comrade O finally resumed his calm, practical tone and democratic simplicity of language. 'Your subordinate is tainted by enemy propaganda. You'll have to look into that mess yourself, Colonel. Take twenty men and go to Lyubimov. Borrow them from the police. We don't want any "menstruations"—everything nice and cultured. No uniforms. Hats and ties like in a restaurant. Just an outing for the lads, a day in the country. No farting out of revolvers unless there's an emergency. A couple of machine-guns won't do any harm, though—take them along. Pick up Makepeace and the other rowdies and bring them in quietly. Re-open the prison and restore telegraphic communications with X. No repression—mind. Order, discipline, legality. Leave the women alone—everything below the tits is out of bounds —no personality cults. You have twenty-four hours to complete the disinfection and I wish you luck. What d'you think, Comrade U?'

'I couldn't agree more, Comrade O. Just one point in connection with the "menstruations" as you so wittily call them. What about rucksacks, fishing rods, balalaikas?—as it's a strictly civic event, something in the nature of a football match or a concert, a country outing with the usual singing and dancing—but no personality cults, as you so rightly say.'

At noon a posse of young men tramped to the station. In spite of the sunny weather they wore black jackets buttoned to the neck and hats jammed down over their sturdy peasant ears; each carried a suitcase in one hand and a balalaika and fishing tackle in the other. Colonel Almazov in gaiters and a topee, a rucksack on his back, was marching on the pavement beside them.

'Sing!'

'Soldiers, brave soldiers,
where are your wives?'
led the red-haired tenor in front.

'Our loaded rifles,
These are our wives,'

73

the chorus took up but soon faltered and broke
off.

'Forgotten your orders?' hissed Almazov.
'Sing a romance!'

> 'I've no nee-ed of a crimson skirt
> Mother, oh, Mother . . .'

the red-head intoned uncertainly. Keeping in
step with difficulty, the unit approached the
station. Three municipal buses were waiting in
a side-street.

'Halt! 'shun! Single file, aboard!'

Bumping their suitcases and dropping their
hats, the men climbed in and relaxed in the
unaccustomed luxury of upholstered passenger
seats, while information was being rapidly
exchanged among the huddle of old women in
the square:

'. . . know what they've got in their suitcases,
love? Loaded rifles and revolvers! . . . And two
machine-guns, two I tell you! . . . They're for-
bidden to touch women below the belt . . . There's
a miraculous ikon been found in Lyubimov . . .
Bishop Leonard . . . He's no bishop, he's Lenny
the innocent, the God's fool . . . He's opening
the churches! He's opening the churches! He's
opening the churches! . . . Help him, O Lord!
Grant him victory, O Lord, over the hosts of
Satan, over the armies of Antichrist . . .'

Meanwhile the people of Lyubimov were enjoy-

ing their holiday and waiting to drink to Makepeace and his young bride who, that very
morning, had been to the registrar's. The
wedding had come as heavenly manna to the
free city which had only been waiting for some
such warm, cheerful occasion to round off its
celebrations of victory. Not that it had been
idle for the past two days—the celebrations had
started on May Day, which had seen the opening
of the new era, but what with so many changes
and upheavals, there hadn't been time really to
get into the swing—and who wanted to count
the days anyway? If Lenny Makepeace had
granted freedom to Lyubimov, it was only right
to celebrate, and what's the use of freedom to a
Russian if he is not to have his fling and enjoy
himself to the damnation of his soul, the terror
of his enemies, and for something to remember
at the hour of his death ?

We Russians are not fond of tippling amateur-
ishly, in solitude, each in his corner, a teaspoonful
at a time. We leave this kind of thing to for-
eigners, to Americans in America and Frenchmen
in France, to drunkards who drink in order to
befuddle their brains and then to sleep it off like
pigs. What we drink for is to fire our souls and
to feel we are alive. It's when we drink that we
come to life, our spirit rises above inert matter
and soars into the empyrean—and what we need
for this exercise is a street, a crooked small-town
street with its hump rising into the white sky.

As a result the street, when Leonard and Serafima came out from the registrar's, was almost unrecognisable. All down the length of Volodarsky Avenue, tables had been set up in a row, covered with white cloths and laden with whatever Providence had sent. Admittedly this wasn't very much, but all the same there were pies and salads, and jellies and vodka, for on this occasion everyone had given of his best.

Yet no one had started eating or drinking : they were all waiting politely, sitting at the ready and passing the time of day. When the newly-weds appeared on the doorstep they were greeted by a delegation of notables with the traditional offering of a bread loaf (a symbol of abundance) and two small glasses as an appetiser. They received the congratulations of the community and its wishes for the success of their married life, but there were no vulgar shouts from the public, no coarse references to their marital needs and no stupid songs or ditties of a pagan origin. Everything was as it should be—cultured, simple and dignified.

The couple on their side behaved as modestly as if they were just like anyone else. The only concessions Leonard had made to the occasion were a pair of mouse-coloured gloves and a paper chrysanthemum in his buttonhole, while Serafima Petrovna hadn't even bothered with a wedding dress (a symbol of chastity) but had only put on a light-coloured blouse and was carrying a decorated sunshade which gave her the air of a princess taking a stroll. Arm-in-arm with her prince, she gazed with intoxicated eyes at his profile.

'Look, Leonard! A loaf! And two glasses! How deligthfully Russian! We must drink a toast and kiss *bruderschaft*!' She laughed wantonly. But Leonard picked up a glass in his gloved hand, sniffed, frowned and put it down.

'Savages!' he growled. 'What's this brew? And what kind of a wedding breakfast is this? Vodka and gherkins! Where are the signs of our prosperity? Disgraceful! What will they say in Europe? Call the managers of the shop, the warehouse and the restaurant.'

The three sheepish-looking officials were already there. They hastened to explain their predicament. There was a shortage of alcohol and no flour, sausage, confectionery or tinned food, butter or meat. There was no fish either and the margarine was running out. The food trust was in the red.

Breaking down before Leonard's searching gaze, the manager of the shop did burst into tears and confess to having a case of toilet soap and two of Borderguard Toffee under the counter, but this was merely a drop in the ocean. As for the warehouse, apart from unbroached supplies of Kharkov mineral water and an imported red pepper so hot that no one had dared touch it with his bare lips for the past three years, all it had was toothpaste, matches, axle grease and Vitamin C tablets useful in cases of anaemia.

'Distribute everything to the population! Charge it to my account!' Makepeace instructed the petrified officials. 'Well, what are you waiting for? Can't you see that the people want to celebrate? Can't you see they want to drink the health of my lawfully wedded wife, Serafima Petrovna? Here she is, I commend her to your loyal affection ... Today the people shall be my guests.'

A strange expression briefly contorted his face.

'Bring that Kharkov drink which has been so neglected by the public. I should like you to taste it, Dr Linde, and tell everyone what its chemical composition is.'

Dr Linde stepped forward from among Leonard's suite and cautiously tipping the bottle, drop by drop, filled a tablespoon with the Kharkov water, well known for its property of softening the walls of the stomach without slaking the thirst of the heart or mind. Hundreds of eyes watched him as, with craned neck and bristling moustache, he sipped it, coughed, licked the spoon, looked at it and finally announced in a tone of utter conviction :

'It's not medicinal water at all! It's pure medicinal alcohol!'

Yes, the medicinal water had turned into medicinal alcohol! In reality it was the same

Kharkov water it had always been, but its effect and therefore its role, its social function, had changed. Under the action of Leonard's influence everyone who tasted it experienced to the full the organic shock and the burning sensation of swallowing pure alcohol and, coughing and spluttering, each in turn exclaimed :

' That's what I call a drink ! It goes through you like a flame and it blossoms in your mouth like a rose ! It's a shame to eat gherkins with it. What it needs is smoked salmon or sturgeon or sucking pig or, better still, a slice of that small-calibre pre-war Crakow salami—just the thought of it turns your spit into mayonnaise and oils your mouth so that you have to be careful not to swallow your tongue ! '

Scarcely had the workers made their wishes known when a banquet of magical splendour appeared on the tables before them. So abrupt and unaccountable was the transformation that a man with a gherkin in his mouth, convinced to the core of his being that he was tasting salami, spat it out, shouting blue murder :

' Help ! It's salami ! Look, look ! It's salami ! '

People stuffed themselves and wept, and mumbled with their mouths full, praising Leonard's princely generosity and kindness. Chopped cabbage tasted of pickled pork, roast potatoes were as fresh and velvety as peaches ; best of all was the red pepper, redder and juicier than the best steak and served in such abundance that some of the revellers quite lost their head and started chucking it to the dogs under the table— but this was sheer waste, for the animals, their wolfish nature unchanged, fled at the sight of it with their tail between their legs.

'Eat! Drink! Don't stint yourselves,' Leonard invited his guests with a wide gesture of his gloved hand. 'I have sufficient supplies to last us for ten years. To each according to his need!'*

Arm in arm with his young bride and followed by his retinue, he progressed at a ceremonial pace, pausing now and then to help someone to an extra portion of eggplant salad, or to create the illusion of a dance band and encourage people to dance, or to pull a guest up or tick another one off, everywhere contributing to the joyful yet seemly mood of the gathering, and achieving all this without the use of his hands—merely by a scarcely perceptible nod or a twitch of the eyebrows.

In order to control the city, Leonard had no need to tear himself in pieces by trying to be everywhere at once. He employed scouts, children who patrolled the streets singly or in groups, and who imparted to the information service the air of an enjoyable game which

---

* Part of Marxist slogan defining Communism: 'From each according to his strength, to each according to his need.'

incidentally trained their faculties and stimulated their curiosity. Twenty of them were posted in the attics and watched over the outskirts of the city. Others acted as messengers to report on incidents caused by social friction.

'Uncle Lenny, Uncle Lenny!' a small boy would gallop up to Makepeace. 'There's a stranger pawing Auntie Dasha in the Guryevs' back yard!'

Leonard rewarded him with a piece of Border-guard Toffee or a nourishing Vitamin C pill, and directed his mental gaze at the Guryevs' back yard. Instantly, the drunken lout let go of his defenceless victim and apologised: 'I'm terribly sorry, Miss. I promise on my honour I won't do it again.' And the rescued girl, instead of making a scene, smiled modestly and said: 'Please don't worry. It's nothing. Would you like my address and my photo?' So the scandal was nipped in the bud.

'Hi, Lenny! Do me a favour—have them serve me some Astrakhan roach, it's years since I've had any!'

A rumbustious old body pranced into the middle of the road, hitching up her long peasant skirt. Drunk as a lord and only kept from soaring into the empyrean by the weight of her huge boots, as knobbly as a ploughed field, she stood swaying like a tree in the wind and whining for roach, as though without it she didn't care whether she lived or died.

81

'All right, Matryona, you'll get your roach.'
He picked up a dry crust but, remembering that
roach was a great rarity in our district and
deciding that the substitute ought to be something as improbable as a woman in a pulpit, he
put it down and drew a tube of toothpaste from
his pocket instead.

'Where's its head?' Matryona was surprised.

'Don't be silly! It's paste, fish paste. No head,
no bones. Can't you see it says "toothpaste"?
It's specially made for toothless people like you.'
Unscrewing the cap and squeezing out a thick
spiral, he spread it on a soft piece of bread.
'There, old lady, eat and enjoy yourself, and
remember Leonard Makepeace.'

His face was pale with fatigue, his forehead
glittered harshly with sweat. The jollier and
rowdier was the merrymaking the deeper his
frown and the sharper the gaze of his crossed[1]
grey eyes, thrust into the crowd like scissor
blades. Alone preoccupied with untimely care,
he kept hotting up the pace, yet glancing at his
watch as though anxious to have the party over
by sundown.

'Attention! A special announcement! For
exactly thirty minutes the river Lyubimovka will
flow with champagne. The champagne, of the
make "Soviet Champagne", is of the highest

---

[1] An eye to an eye—you need that with our
people.

grade. Those who've never had any should consult their neighbours. There is nothing to be afraid of—this is a new technical discovery : I am simply diverting the course of the river so that it will run with champagne. Remember : thirty minutes precisely from when I say go. Now! Go! No! Stop! Wait! You'll trample each other to death, you savages! Children are not to drink. Invalids are to have priority. Use glasses. Don't wade in or you'll drown. And where d'you think you're going, Savely Kuzmich? Come back at once. Your place, and Dr Linde's, is here with me.'

'I only wanted a sip, just to see what our rotten little river could produce, it wouldn't take a minute!' Forgetting his duty and dignity as our historiographer, Proferansov had been swept away by the surge of the unenlightened crowd. 'Look at them!' He pointed at the bank echoing with cries and splashes and at the golden spray of champagne flying to the clouds. "Why can't I go, Comrade Makepeace? Do let me, Serafima Petrovna. Why this discrimination? Aren't I a human being[1]?'

'Human beings!' muttered Leonard. Suddenly dizzy, he closed his eyes. 'Am I drunk

---

[1] Lies! I never wanted to go. And why should I suddenly be 'he' in my own book? Aren't I a human being?

like all these ignorant, weak, foolish people ? '
he asked himself. ' Or am I alone drunk, while
all the rest of the world is sober ? Could I be
the only victim of my own hypnosis ? Intoxicated by my crazy dream, have I imagined all
this ?—the wedding breakfast, the shouts by the
river—and my easy victory over a woman so
recently indifferent to my love . . .'

' You look ill,' Serafima exclaimed anxiously.
' Have something. A drink ? A sandwich ?
Some fish paste ? '

' *No* ! ' He pulled himself together. ' We'll
have something at home,' he said more calmly,
squinting round at his depleted retinue ' Let's
go for a stroll, my friends—we'll walk up to the
monastery ruins and have a look at the view
from above. Away from this smell . . . It's the
fumes of the champagne . . . Of course it's no
temptation to us, leaders and people in responsible positions—we don't want it, we don't like it
—is that understood ? You, Proferansov, should
be the last to go scampering off after wine and
spirits like a schoolboy[1]. Your task as a
writer, as the historian of our city, is to observe
reality in its unwavering march towards the
future and faithfully to record each event. Be
our mirror, Proferansov, be our Leo Tolstoy—
it's no wonder he is known among the people as
the mirror of the Revolution. Look at life

---

[1] Ever since, I have kept strictly to beer.

around you, soak yourself in it, and be its living reflection in your memoirs.'

The chaotic city, abandoned to its Bacchic frenzy, lay spread before them like a patchwork quilt. White tablecloths, red flags and purple skirts billowed in the wind, clashing with the tender green of the young fields running their wedges from the skyline into the valley and cutting across the bare, steely-looking woods. Add to this the winding, branching, bottle-coloured river, the townsfolk clustering along its banks, the narrow, twisting streets and alleys and the lop-sided church with crows wheeling around its broken dome ; the graveyard like a sampler in faded cross-stitch, the yellow hospital shaped like a coffin and, next to it, the brownish-red rectangular block of the prison; add the waste plot with its mounds of rubbish and the empty highway streaked silver with mud, the belfry, the fences, the scuffling dogs, the wail of a concertina, the curl of smoke rising from a chimney and the clouds racing like horses with flowing manes—add and mix, and you will have the picture which lay before the eyes of Makepeace and his suite.

' Truly, a picture worthy of the artist's brush ! ' Proferansov took a deep breath. ' Behold the fulfilment of the people's century-old dream. Behold the rivers of milk and honey, the King-dom of Heaven which in scientific terms is the great leap forward! Never before in the history of the world has the individual received such care, never before . . .'

'Thank you, my dear fellow, that's enough for now. Write it down for me.' Makepeace patted him on the shoulder. At a sign from him his companions withdrew to a distance of forty paces, leaving him with his lovely bride.

'You understand, dearest, it wouldn't have been a good thing to let Savely blurt out all my ideas, but what he was inspired to say just now had a good deal in it. Do you remember, darling, that I once promised you the city of Lyubimov? No, don't argue—you can't refuse my wedding gift. Well, there it lies, meek and submissive at our feet. Meek and yet—think of it—free and independent as well, a happy city, happy because I direct all its thoughts and desires. The people have the rarest food and drink at their disposal, free of charge and incidentally without danger to their health, yet they have no oppressive feeling of dependence—they trust us completely, they love us like children. I could make them hew stones and dig drainage ditches, but I don't want to. They are my fellow citizens, I make allowances even for their weaknesses. No one in our city shall ever again be hungry or ill or sad. And to begin with, tell me, darling, are you pleased? Are you happy?'

'So happy,' she whispered, blushing becomingly and pressing her face to his heaving breast. 'So proud and grateful, my love. At last we are united, at last you have claimed me for your own before the face of the whole city [1]! But without you, dearest, what use to me would be the city, or the world itself? How could I, how could I, ever have been so foolish as to under-estimate you! You with your genius, your goodness, your charm, your looks . . .'

She was about to melt in his arms when he hastily stepped aside.

'Wait. Look. Messengers. Two of them . . . Something must have happened.—Well, what is it? What's the matter with them now?'

'Uncle Lenny, Uncle Lenny, a stranger has died in Dyatlov's field . . .'

Makepeace frowned.

'What's this? Died? Who said he could die? Or was it . . . did he have a fatal disease? Was he very old?'

'No, he wasn't old,' the boy chattered excitedly. 'The men are saying he died of drink. Got sozzled on pure spirits, they say—drank it neat.'

The crowd of onlookers parted respectfully. Dr Linde, down on one knee beside the body, put away his stethoscope.

'Well, there's nothing science can do for him.' He got up. 'No mystery about his death either. He stinks of alcohol exactly like that bottle you

---

[1] The more fool he when he could have got whatever he wanted for nothing!

87

gave me to taste. Not even the strongest constitution could stand up to two litres of that remarkable drink, believe me ! '

' Come off it,' Leonard wanted to say. ' I know how much alcohol there is in a bottle of Kharkov water, and there's none to be had in town even on a prescription.' But he only asked :

' Did anyone know this man ? "

No one knew him.

The man lay flat on his back, palms up, like an image of Christ. The men had evidently tried to revive him but given it up and merely turned him over to see who it was. The features had not yet had time to set and they and, still more, the inextinguishable brightness of the blue football shirt and the trousers with their herringbone seams (one leg rucked up and showing the laces of the modest proletarian pants) emphasised the sad equality in destitution of all men before the brisk and workmanlike hand of death. Makepeace thought of checking the doctor's statement that the dead man smelt of alcohol but for some reason his courage failed him and he only stared at the herringbone seams and the dirty feet in their canvas shoes.

' I know who that is,' said Proferansov. ' It's that thief you let out of prison yesterday. Don't you remember ? He was there with the three others you insisted on seeing personally to hand them their amnesty. He's not one of our lads,

88

goodness knows how he got into our prison—probably stepped off on his way to Siberia ! It was a bad idea to let him out. They ought to be shot or hanged, people like that.'

' So that's who you are,' Leonard muttered as the image of the prisoner in the blue football shirt revived in his memory. At first he had done nothing but whine : ' Give us a cig, Guv, give us extra rations for May Day, Guv, it's the custom, Guv.' Then suddenly, as if reading an item in a newspaper, he had announced in a loud, clear voice that, being in Melitopol, he had had the luck to pinch a gold watch from a barmaid —an ill-considered action which he now regretted as he wished to amend his criminal ways.

' From now on, live up to your human dignity,' Makepeace had adjured them at the open gate of the prison. ' Don't kill, don't steal, don't forge documents, don't commit crimes which degrade you as human beings. Remember the noble sound of the word " man "*'.

' And now what ? ' he mentally addressed his disappointing pupil. ' I let you out, I give you back your life and liberty, I invite you to the common table, I try to make a man of you, and all you do in return is drink yourself to death and spoil the day for everyone else ! I suppose, if I'd left you under lock and key, you'd still be sitting on your bunk, gambling with your friends

* Reference to a famous quotation from Gorky.

and drinking the bitter vodka you paid the jailor the eyes out of your head for, and you wouldn't have a care in the world—is that what you're telling me? Well, what do you expect me to do now? Put everyone behind bars and watch them through the spy hole? Wait, let me think . . . It was freedom you say you wanted? But why, when I'd already given you more than enough? Was it freedom from your own life, from your own mind and your dangerous human flesh which becomes so light and buoyant when you are drunk that you seem to jump out of yourself and hover outside it like a ghost? Well, have you got what you wanted? Are you free at last?'

He squatted on his heels and, overcoming his revulsion, bent over the dead mouth. It smelled of nothing.

'Yes, I see,' he muttered. 'I see. Well, perhaps you're right. Perhaps there's something I've overlooked.'

'Leonard, I beg of you,' Serafima crooned. It's a bad omen. Do resurrect him.'

He leapt up, shaking with fury.

'Are you all out of your minds? Do you take me for a miracle worker?'

'Couldn't you, just to please me?'

Her question remained unanswered because at this moment there came the warning of an armed attack upon the city, and the drunkard's leap to life was instantly forgotten. From all sides, the ears of the citizens were blasted by the shrill Pioneer whistles of the scouts in the attics.*

'At last!' cried Leonard, bounding up the hill and devouring the distance with his eyes. 'O envious bureaucrats! I was awaiting your attack!—Lucky they've come by day. At least, we can see the enemy.'

Three suspicious looking buses were trundling along the winding highway across the fields. Watching them through his fieldglasses, Makepeace whispered his instructions to the population :

'The party is over. Everyone is to sober up, pull himself together and make himself tidy. Clear the tables and bring them in off the streets. Take down the flags. The city may be shelled, anyone who suffers from nerves is to go to bed and sleep. The scouts in the attics will stay at their posts and report to me personally the appearance of any more vehicles, cavalry or infantry.'

Bent double and running from cover to cover, Proferansov reached the top of the bluff and took shelter behind the Commander.

'Didn't I tell you not to get rid of those weapons?' he hissed, panting. 'What are we going to shoot with now? How can we repel the aggressor who dares to meddle in our affairs?

* Pioneers are the junior branch of the Communist Youth League.

I told you it was too soon for complete dis-armament. Now you'll see . . . We'll lose the battle.'

One after the other, the buses rolled into the valley, skirting the dark, metallic-looking scrub. Clamped to his fieldglasses, the Commander stood motionless. Only his back quivered and a hysterically joyful note exploded in his voice:

'Don't panic, Savely. We are not going to shed blood. There won't be any more corpses. The death of the sodden parasite was enough. Let him be the only victim of our struggle against the past—the past is over and done with. And now stop fidgeting behind my back like a clown. Go away, old chap, you're getting on my nerves. Go home, all of you. Lock your doors, stuff your windows with cushions and sit tight. Pretend you are in prison—for a time, of course, and for your own good. Tell Serafima Petrovna to lie down and not to worry. Off you go. I don't need your help, I need to be alone to concentrate.'

At the foot of the hill, Proferansov stopped and looked up. His back against the jagged monastery wall, Makepeace stood gazing sternly into the distance. His eyes seemed to emit blue flashes. Had it been dark, they would no doubt have blazed like the eyes of jungle animals at night. But the sun was still high up and, as it dived in and out of the white clouds, its inter-

mittent rays illuminated the lonely figure of the
Commander at the top of the bluff.

' Well, why aren't we getting a move on, driver ?
Didn't I tell you in plain Russian : full steam
ahead to the city centre and pull up in front of
the post office, which is next to the monastery ? '

' It's stalled, Comrade Lieutenant-Colonel. The
carburettor is playing up.'

Almazov cursed and got out. The city was
within a stone's throw but all three buses had
stopped and the drivers had their sleeves rolled
up and were fiddling with the engines. The fiend
in charge of the last one was for some reason
taking off a front wheel.

After walking round them in circles and prom-
ising them fifteen days in quod, Almazov gave
it up as a bad job.

' Hop out, we'll go on foot. Now remember:
this is a picnic—a day out in the country and
a chance to see some interesting national monuments. Put your hat on, Sergeant, and button
up your jacket. And don't forget the machine
guns.'

The road looped its way through scrub and
turned off into a stunted copse, as misty and
deserted as in winter. Rusty remnants of last
year's grass crunched and squelched in the sodden
ground under their feet. Stumps and uprooted
trees reared on every side, and black boles shot

up inches away in front, like pillars of mud spurting from shell holes.

'Halt! Where's the road? About turn!'

They turned, but within a quarter of an hour the Colonel knew that they were lost—lost in a small copse on the edge of the town they had already caught a glimpse of on their way through the scrub! It seemed impossible that a hundred yards to the right or left the forest shouldn't open on a view of roofs and fences, and the once famous Lyubimov Monastery. Hidden by the folds of the terrain, the city lay so close that Almazov could hear the dogs barking and the cocks crowing in its back yards. Every now and then he actually smelled the smoke from a chimney stack and hopefully attacked a new path, only to wear out his men who were sweltering in the civilian elegance of their unseasonable clothes.

'Comrade Lieutenant-Colonel,' the Sergeant smacked his hand into the brim of his felt hat, 'may I say something? I think it must be Leshy who's leading us astray*.'

'What Leshy?'

'Leshy, Lenny—the wizard who rules over these boggy parts. He's been leading us in circles to keep us away from his lair.'

'Don't talk rubbish! Get your weapons ready.'

* Leshy: (from *les*—forest), the spirit of the woods in Russian folklore.

94

But scarcely had they unpacked their two machine guns and begun to assemble one of them when a grunting, crashing noise came from the undergrowth and something unnamable flew up with a heart-rending screech of pain and burst into high shivers of laughter above the trembling tree-tops.

' Halt ! Who goes there ? ' shouted the Colonel. ' Halt or I'll shoot.' But already he and his panic-stricken unit were fleeing through the savage woods, abandoning their weapons and scattering hats, fishing rods and balalaikas as they ran as fast as their legs would carry them.

What were they running from at the risk of drowning in a quagmire or putting out their eyes on a twig ? If you asked them today, not one of them could tell you. Only perhaps in another three score years and ten will a one-eyed centenarian tell his children's children and grandchildren the story of the totally unexpected misfortune which overtook the platoon in the woods—adding for their edification that no one since the beginning of time has yet been able to account for the ways of the Evil One. Why for instance should he howl in the chimney on a winter night, or scrabble under the floorboards, or moan in an inhuman voice over the moors, only to add to the burden of sadness already weighing upon a man's heart ?

It's the wind that howls, and the mice that scratch, and there's a woodland bird that moans when it mourns its young, the children will say in the belief that everything can be explained.

'But why should you think your Grandfather is a fool?' the centenarian will reply. 'Do you really think that a man who has survived the third and the fourth world wars and has only lost one eye in all his years of service (and that only through running his head into a fir tree)—do you really believe that such a man can't tell the sound of the wind or of mice from some other sound? Believe me, I've learned more about mice than you have about logarithms, and if I speak of such things at all, I do it with a fine sense of distinctions. A mouse is a mouse—and the woodland bird, if you want to know, is a bittern—but the Power of Evil is something else again, and you can't explain it away. And when a man is suddenly seized with a choking, inexplicable terror, it's because the devil himself is rushing away with him through the woods, no one knows whither, to mock and torment him until he has tired of the game.

'No, my children, your forefathers were not as naive as you like to believe, and if you have never experienced that fear and confusion for yourselves, it's only because you are young and foolish. And yet the paths behind you are already tangled and overgrown, and instead of the cosy villas you expected to see there are nothing but blackened stumps around you, and trees rising in front of you like fountains of cascading mud.

And any moment now, a strange cry will ring out in the darkness and you will take to your heels—and God help you then, and keep you away from the quagmires.'

Almazov sat down on the trunk of a fallen elm. It was sultry. He could feel the smell of the rotting stumps and of his own torn and sweat-soaked clothes and boots. It drizzled in spurts ; the rain dried immediately in the sun. A mushroom rain he would have called it in August, but this was the spring mating season, the season of the early courtship of moorfowl— and wasn't it strange, it suddenly occurred to him, that in such a glorious month there shouldn't be a single flutter or chirrup in the trees ?

Scarcely had the thought stirred sluggishly in his brain, reaching him through a drowsy mist and leaving him passive and resigned, when he noticed a bird with an outsize head sitting on a branch above him. It was muddy-green and looked like nothing so much as a very large and well-fed toad.

' What a monster ! It's more like a crocodile ! ' he said to himself, but without the slightest temptation to reach for his gun. He merely observed the fact of its nearness—and although he already dimly realised that it was to the cry of this very bird that he owed the ineffaceable blot on his honour as an officer, he felt no shame, no fear and no regret as he sank into an almost sensuous contemplation of the hideous creature

97

sitting on its bough in the sun and watching him with the eyes of a snake.

'What would a scientist say to this fright if I brought it back as a specimen?' He knew that the question was academic—not because he doubted his capacity to get up and look for the vanished path, but because it seemed pointless : why go to so much trouble merely to resume the burdensome freedom of existence ? Why not meekly give up his will, if only to this monster, whose poisoned gaze was pouring apathy into his soul and licking his tormented brain smooth with its deliciously tranquillising caress ? He had lived well and worked hard, he deserved a rest. Why not 'rest in peace' as they say on such occasions ?

More for the sake of tidiness than out of vanity, he unhurriedly listed his various merits and achievements — the many gangs, nests, centres, sects and conspiracies, by now a little confused in his memory, which he had unmasked and liquidated in the course of his industrious life. And he gratefully remembered the many lovely women who had loved him and whose love he had returned for a brief, happy and tempestuous season. Except for the more retarded, though still delightful, of the simple village girls, they had all for some reason adopted his romantic style and addressed him as *mon amour* and *mon colonel*, though without always achieving his perfection of accent. Now their houri

98

voices no longer stirred his blood, they were merely lulling him to sleep. Without any urgency—almost only out of a male code of civility and obligation—he now summoned the loveliest of them to a passing out parade, but found himself confusing the records and combining Vava's breasts with Zina's tresses and both with the queenly thighs of Zhenya who had been haunting him in recent months.

The bird was beginning to show signs of impatience. It stretched and shook its powerful webbed wings, craned its neck and, without removing its eyes from Almazov's, strutted a few steps along the branch. Opening its beak, it revealed a row of fish's teeth.

' Do birds have teeth ? ' he tried to remember, but not very hard. He realised perfectly that the merciful drug he had taken an hour earlier was quietly and painlessly at work in his chilling veins, and that perhaps the bird, which he regarded with increasing respect, was only waiting for its carrion feast. He could have brought it down with a single shot, but it would have meant getting his gun out of his rucksack where Sophie had carefully packed it, together with his silver soap dish and scented towel. After all, it was rather chivalrous of the bird to wait politely instead of harrying him—perhaps it even felt a measure of unspoken sympathy . . . No longer able to move his tongue, he addressed it mentally in French, bestowing on it the familiar terms of endearment he had once showered upon his fair charmers, and the bird seemed to nod understandingly—but he knew that this was only a delusion induced by the drug. At the very end, it opened its large, toothy maw and said a little hoarsely but in perfect Parisian : ' *Merci, mon amour, vous m'avez fait très grand plaisir, mon brave colonel.*'

Chapter Four

Visitors

~~~~~~

The city of Lyubimov vanished as if the earth had swallowed it. Again and again expeditions were sent out and every foot of ground was gone over with a map and calipers—where a flourishing city had once stood there was nothing but wasteland, bog and craters which the spring floods had filled with mud. 'There must have been a geological subsidence,' the authorities finally decided after consulting experts. 'The moisture left over from the ice age came up through the cracks, and the city and the few insignificant villages around it were sucked under.'[1]

---

[1] In reality the city was protected by an electric signalling system. A zone with a twenty mile radius was surrounded by cables and any uninvited guest who stepped across the border was announced to the C. in C. by bells ringing

'All we want is a breathing space, a year of peace.' Makepeace was striding up and down his study. 'By then our economy will have outshone Belgium, outstripped Holland—we can begin to think about territorial expansion and the propagation of our ideas on a mass scale. Not by lies or violence—only by the living force of our example and our influence over progressive minds do we intend to gain the recognition and the sympathy of the world. Put that down, Proferansov. Make a note of it in the record of our struggles and achievements.'

A labour unit was setting off to dig a drainage ditch. Leaving Proferansov to his job, Makepeace hurried out on to the balcony to speed them on their way.

'Heads higher! Shoulders back! Smile! Sing! Remember, no one forces you to work. It's you who want to overfulfil your norm by two hundred per cent. Yes, yes, two hundred, no less! Your hearts are uplifted, your arms are full of strength, you long to thrust your picks into the soil!'

---

and lights flashing at his H.Q. Ever at his post, Makepeace turned the intruder away by directing his will power at the appropriate square on the map. What he didn't know was that, before the system had been set up, two secret agents coming from different directions had slipped inside the zone where they were now lying low.

After the digging party had sprinted off to the assault of its citadel of clay, he sank back, exhausted, in his armchair.

'And yet, you know, it's never the norms or the economic levels that have priority in my system: always the individual comes first. Thanks to my leadership, even the hard manual work of these men becomes a creative task—so far from crushing their spirit, it fills them with the triumphant sense of their titanic might and the inspired urge to rival the labours of Hercules. I, alone, in utter solitude, must bear the burden of care, doubt, worry, dissatisfaction. And on top of that . . . do I really have to put up with this caterwauling?'

The 'caterwauling' was coming from the drawing-room where Serafima Petrovna was tempestuously singing and playing the piano. In spite of the thick walls of the old mansion, the sound occasionally reached Leonard in his apartment, especially when the lovely woman in her romantic mood attacked a passage from *Carmen*:

L'amour est enfant de Bohème
Il n'a jamais connu de lois . . .

The whole force of her young, unbridled temperament went into the words, and the stirring melody rang out again and again as she tried it this way and that—

L'amour? L'amou-our!
L'amour? L'amou-our!
L'amour! L'amourl'amourl'amour l'a-mour!. .

reaching its climax in Carmen's challenge to her
inconstant lover:

Si tu ne m'aimes pas je t'aime
Et si je t'aime prends garde à toi!

Short of a timely intervention by Leonard, the
performance ended in an attack of nerves. The
lid slammed down, the keys jangled, and peal
upon peal of raucous laughter rang out in the
empty rooms. Proferansov sighed and glanced
covertly at Makepeace who frowned and, tearing
himself away from his task of leadership, mentally
addressed his wife through the wall, giving her
permission to enter. Pale, controlled, dressed
in the expensive clothes she had worn all day,
she appeared in the doorway and gazed at him
with radiant adoration.

'You called me, Leonard? I'm sorry, I've disturbed you again by practising that passage from
Bizet. Don't be cross, darling. I'm very happy,
only I miss you a little. You slept in the study
again and you didn't say good night to me . . .
Forgive me, I don't mean . . . Just let me kiss
you . . .'

He held her soothingly in his arms and for a
moment dutifully nibbled the edge of her delicate
ear lobe. 'How can I afford this,' he thought
wretchedly as he gently checked her persistence.
'The city, the individual, the currency reform,
the spring-sowing . . . And when did I last spend
an undisturbed night? Every time a hare or an

104

owl crosses the border, I sit up, sweating. Not a
moment's peace . . . And on top of that this
puppet expects me to spend time and energy
amusing her . . . Couldn't she wait a bit? Why
I ever made her fall in love with me . . .'

But to douse the flame he had deliberately set
alight was more than he felt like doing. He held
her at arm's length, as delicately as if she were
made of china:

'Why don't you take up a hobby, Sima darling?
Culture, morals, the family—all that side of things
I leave to you . . . Now run along, my dear, and
don't worry. I'll be in to dinner. I'm busy now,
you can see, there are people waiting to see me.
Run along.'

Happy once again, she ran along.[1]

From early morning on, there were people
queuing in the yard, waiting to see Makepeace.
He asked himself whether it wouldn't be better
to drop the time-honoured Russian custom of
allowing everyone to take all his problems, however trifling, straight to the Tsar, but decided that
it was easier to rule a kingdom if the needs and

---

[1] 'My dear, I don't know how you do it—if it
were me, I'd have died of fright,' confessed the
wife of the headmaster of the school where
Serafima's competence had only been regarded
as average. 'It isn't every woman who could live
up to the expectations of a man of genius. I can
imagine—his passion, his whims! It must be

preoccupations of the subjects were brought openly before the ruler. Not that the question of their needs ever arose for he knew them better than did his visitors. Say, for instance, that a widow came to petition him for reeds to mend the thatched roof of her barn. —Treating her like a duchess, he first put her in the best armchair, then he gave her a look of astonishment:

'Thatch? For a barn? Whoever heard of a thatched roof on a twentieth century barn! Wouldn't you prefer tiles? or at least corrugated iron? though I think sheet zinc would really be best. But is this really all you came to see me about? Are you sure there's nothing else on your mind? I wonder now . . . Isn't it a fact that you are sick of looking after your two sheep and your calf, all as greedy as rats—you've had enough of

---

like a fairytale, like being caged with a tiger. Why, even I—goodness knows I'm happily married, I'm older, I've got five children—yet quite honestly, every time I catch sight of him I nearly pass out! I can just imagine—to meet the demands of his questing soul, you have to be on your toes like a ballerina at the Bolshoi. Don't tell me but take my advice—don't let any young woman get anywhere near him. Great men are particularly sensitive to beauty and what young woman could refuse him anything.' Serafima only sighed mysteriously.

small scale farming and you would like to hand your farm stock over to the State? You feel you are wasting your time, carting hay and manure, when you could be using it to study the internal combustion engine which, as you know, will soon be running up and down our fields with emancipated woman at the wheel. Have I guessed your secret wish, Citizeness? Tell me.'

'You have indeed! You've hit the nail on the head! You've sorted out the combustion engine of my soul,' cried the widow, ten years younger at the thought of the new prospects before her. 'Take my roosters and my pig as well, they're nothing but a nuisance to me. They are obstacles to my cultural development. To hell with them! I want to be a tractor driver, I want to wear trousers and sit at the wheel. Where's my tractor?'

'Not so fast, Citizeness!' Leonard had to check the zeal he had aroused in the retarded woman's breast. 'Your roosters you'd better keep for the present, or how will you feed your fatherless children until such time as the State has tripled the rations, which it soon will, of course? The pig we'll add to the list of your voluntary contributions—put it down, Proferansov. What did you say its name was, Citizeness? Boris? Excellent. Now if you'd just sign for Boris and the calf and the sheep. We have to keep track of everything, you know, down to the smallest cog, especially in view of the international situation and the danger of capitalist encirclement.'[1]

'Next!' Leonard called out. 'Come in!' The next moment he sat up at the sight of his visitor. Arms akimbo, there stood before him a typical Western tourist—such as we had never yet set eyes on in our backward town, though we had heard plenty about their ways and methods—a tourist in a leather jacket, crumpled shorts and yellow shoes with rubber soles, a camera dangling on his stomach, his legs shamelessly exposed and his teeth bared in a hypocritical American smile.

'Allow me to introduce myself, Herr Makepeace,' he godlessly mispronounced our beautiful language. '*Ich bin* Harry Jackson, correspondent of the bourgeois paper *Perdit Intriguer Och Aus America*. My transatlantic masters have sent me to ask you for an interview.'

Sprawling in the best armchair like a colt in a stable, he lit a fat black cigar like a dry stick of manure and proceeded to ask one provocative question after another. How soon would the

---

[1] He had yet to learn that he had lost track of two cogs, or rather two birds from across the border who had gone to ground in the city. One was the famous universal agent from Moscow, Vitaly Kochetov, sent on orders from the Centre. The other was a very different kettle of fish. But let him speak for himself.

corrupt régime of capitalist bosses be established in Lyubimov, he was anxious to know.

'When the lobsters have learned to whistle,' was the brief and unequivocal reply.

And was there any truth in the rumour of an armed clash between the Centre and ourselves?

'Dogs bark, the wind carries the noise,' Leonard made short work of this attempt at interference in our family affairs.

Finally, when the journalist suggested that we should join NATO and take part in the intrigues instigated by Washington, Lenny, calm and dignified, made an obscene gesture which the foreigner understood at once. He instantly forgot his diplomatic manner, stopped playing the fool and indecently tormenting the language, and got down to business.[1]

---

[1] Meanwhile the universal agent Kochetov, in pre-revolutionary bark shoes and such puttees as are only to be seen in our day on parasites who are divorced from our way of life, was limping along the side street. His face was hidden by the peak of his outsize cap, the cap itself served as an aerial, and the limp was due to the fact that he was tapping out a message with his right heel. To avoid giving away his code, we print it in clear:

Vitaly Kochetov calling. According to my information Dictator Makepeace disposes of an extremely powerful weapon of psycho-

'For God's sake, Lenny, sell us your invention,' Harry Jackson implored, dropping his foreign affectations. 'I'm offering you two million down. For that you can build yourself a palace of pure marble encrusted with gold and keep the mud off the roads within a radius of twenty miles by

---

logical warfare. Have spent past week underground without sleep, almost without food, and trying as advised to think less about sex in order to resist prevailing atmosphere of ideological dissolution. (Damn these potholes! Nearly broke my ankle this time! Those damned deviationists must have mined the roads. Before sending up my report, please attend to inadequacies of style due to field conditions. Message continues.) The city has the property of making itself invisible to the outside world. Method of camouflage still unclear. Suggest locating position with aid of air force. Advise raid by long range bombers. Delay operation until after my arrival. Request instructions, relief, new bearings, may need treatment on my return. Am bearding bear in lair. End of message. Greetings from the front to my beloved wife Katya and to my comrade in arms Anatole Sofronov.
Kochetov switched off and raised his voice in a nasal whine:
'A copeck! Spare a copeck for a poor pilgrim!'

paving them with rubber a yard thick. I only mention this because I nearly got drowned on your Russian roads on my way here. That's why I'm so unsuitably dressed in shorts for my interview with you on matters of state. It's lucky I had my White Fang soap and my Uncle Tom's Cabin boot polish with me from New York, at least I

A boy with a squealing pig on a rope was coming up the street.

'Quiet, Boris! Wait till they start turning you into sausage meat. What is it you want, Citizen? I haven't got a copeck. Don't you know money has been abolished? Leonard Makepeace says "Money is a hindrance. The sooner we forget about it the sooner we'll build up our industry." '

'How am I to know, sonny? I've only just come, straight from my backward village up country. Damn these fleas, they'll be the death of me! Tell me, sonny, why are they doing all this digging and demolishing in your town? I see half the monastery wall is gone. Might they be building a factory of strategic importance? Or may be it's an emplacement for an anti-aircraft battery?'

'No, it's a stadium.'

'A what?'

'A football stadium. Makepeace says, "Everyone has the right to develop his physique." '

'You keep talking about him but where does he hide himself, your Makepeace? Tell me, sonny.

could wash and freshen up before coming to call on you as one gentleman on another. Frankly, I've been watching your secret weapon for the past week and it's a matter of life or death for us to get it. I don't have to tell you, old man, the economic crisis is no joke and the unemployment figures are rising. You can't finish everyone off with atom bombs. As you've discovered, it's much better to grab hold of the minds of the destitute, sit at the wheel of their souls so to speak, and give it a good twist backwards, away from progress. So that's my offer to you, old chap—two million down and I'll stand you a drink as well.'

Leonard itched to slap Jackson's face and wipe

I'm only an ignorant peasant. Is that your pig making this stink?'

'Comrade Makepeace doesn't hide himself from anyone. He works hard all day and all night in that handsome building over there. See those first floor windows on the left? That's his H.Q. Why don't you go and see him, Grandpa? He'll tell you all you need to know. Comrade Makepeace says, "Everyone has the right to moral assistance and advice." '

The boy went his way and Kochetov shinned up the drainpipe to the window of Leonard's study. The curtain billowed but neither Makepeace nor his foreign guest noticed, nor of course did Proferansov, half asleep in his corner.

the smugness off it, to punish him for his insulting remark about progress, but he realised that such an outburst could lead to an international incident and unleash a world war, so he checked the impulse and concentrated instead on the tourist's bourgeois mind. Grabbing it by the throat or perhaps by the wheel, he gave it such a twist that it began at once to refute all its own arguments, clearly showing itself to be no match for a Russian in the field of the critique of pure reason.

Silently, looking as if it had nothing to do with him, Leonard watched the transformation, as the journalist repeated out loud, like a parrot, the lessons he was mentally dictating to him. Proferansov had time to take a few notes on some of the subjects dealt with in the interview, and these may assist future scholars in their study of historical trends:

1. *The part played by roads in the history of Russia.* Certain hostile critics of our country slander our roads and claim that in spring and autumn even lorries drown on them in torrents of mud. Yet we have only to turn back the pages of history to see that this very mud has again and again saved Russia from foreign invasion. Host after host— the Poles, Napoleon, the Germans—all have stuck in our mud—as no doubt they will again.

2. *The role of money in world economics.* There are pseudo-scientists who claim that money is useful as an economic incentive and that it links the satisfaction of man's selfish needs to the amount

of work he is prepared to do. But what becomes of money once the needs themselves are directed and controlled? It becomes a temptation to evil, as when a man needs to become a Hero of Labour and the money in his pocket whispers to him: 'What's the hurry? Have a drink first'.

The abolition of money brings with it a number of immediate social benefits. Firstly, such survivals of the past as drunkenness, over-eating, theft, robbery and other crimes disappear overnight. Secondly, universal happiness dawns upon the world, for instead of rampaging chaotically as before, individual needs are only allowed to arise as and when the planned economy is able to satisfy them!

'Thirdly,' Leonard impatiently prompted out loud.

'Thirdly,' the American babbled on, 'thirdly, no one can sell his country or buy freedom for any number of millions . . .'

'And fourthly!' Rising to his full height, Leonard pointed with a lordly gesture at the walls. 'Fourthly, this is what we do with our accumulated capital!'

'. . . with our accumulated capital.' Jackson looked and uttered a weak groan.[1]

The walls were pasted from top to bottom with hundred-rouble notes. It looked at a first glance

---

[1] Watching through a chink in the curtains, Kochetov also groaned.

like an agreeable wallpaper with a pattern of coloured blobs, but a closer examination revealed that each blob was worth exactly one hundred roubles. Only in the area around the stove (the Treasury having run out of paper currency of the appropriate denomination) did the price go down to twenty-fives (the notes as crisp as if they had just been won in a State lottery) and even to rubbed and greasy fives and threes. The total sum was enormous and the income was continually going up as the gradual process of transition to a non-currency basis hadn't so far been completed.

'You won't get it off, it's stuck fast,' Leonard warned the overseas visitor who at the sight of so much treasure was ready to climb the walls.

With this the journalist, now thoroughly ashamed of himself, was politely given to understand that the audience was over and that if he promised never to spy again he could take himself off to his America just as soon as he liked.

'Convey my greetings to the peace-loving peoples of the Western Hemisphere and tell them they can always count on us in case of need,' Makepeace added before giving Proferansov the order to see Jackson off the premises and to tell them outside that no one else would be received until Thursday.

He needed after this interview to be alone with his thoughts. Like ants in a disturbed antheap, they scurried about in a frenzy of construction, putting up ever loftier sky-scrapers. He pictured

to himself all the greatest powers laying down
their arms and opening their frontiers and the
grateful nations of their own will—without the
slightest compulsion—falling into his arms. He
racked his brain for a new name to bestow upon
Lyubimov the day it was proclaimed the capital
of the world : he hesitated between 'City of the
Sun' and just 'Makepeace'. Then he remembered
that at present his will power had a range of only
twenty miles, and once again became absorbed in
the urgent need for a magnetic magnifier of
unlimited range. 'An instrument of such power
and precision,' he reflected, chewing his lips,
'that without moving from this very room, I'll
shake up the whole of mankind—get it out of its
dead end—and then gradually, in time, undertake
the conquest of the Antarctic and the industrial
exploitation of outer space.' He was mentally
contemplating the image of mankind as a giant
with the torso of a wrestler and the noble head
(in profile) of a thinker (was it not his own
ministerial head?) when on turning his chin he
became annoyingly aware of the presence beside
him of a decrepit little old woman with a familiar
mole on her squashed, creased, peasant face.

'Our Lenny!' she sighed, mumbling toothlessly
and blinking in timid joy. 'Here's a bit of cottage
cheese and sour cream for you, love. You aren't
eating enough . . . Look at you, as thin as a
rake . . . I can see right through you, you're like
a shadow . . .'

She hadn't the nerve to hug him, only her worried eyes kept running nimbly up and down him, as if anxious to feel his grimly emaciated flesh.

'Slipped in through the back door,' Proferansov grumbled apologetically. 'Said she had a parcel for her son. A parcel, I ask you! You'd think it was a prison! There's a mother all over for you!' —a woman without an idea in her head except to feed, to press an extra morsel on her darling child! The child may have grown up to be a member of the Cabinet or the ruler of the world for all she cares—she'll shuffle straight into the royal palace, her feet in their torn galoshes and her worthless present done up in a handkerchief, just as if he were neither a philosopher nor a king but a homeless, hungry, hunted puppy.

'Make yourself at home, Mama. What can I do for you?'

He drew up the armchair which he used to impress his petitioners, but he couldn't get any sense out of her, however hard he tried. She could talk of nothing but trifles and domestic details. 'Have a little cottage cheese . . . The sink has come off the wall again and there's no one to fix it up . . .' Hadn't anyone explained to her his political role in the world of today? . . . Yet she must have heard something and no doubt interpreted it in her own way for she let slip:

'You shouldn't hurt the monastery, Lenny love.

117

It wasn't you who built it and it's not for you to pull it down . . .'

This was more than he could take with a straight face:

'Really, Mama, your own son is very nearly ruling the stars and you talk about God! That you of all people should come to me with such fables—it would amuse me if it were not so sad! You're not a stranger to me after all, remember, you are my mother, you must try to consider my position—and couldn't you grow up a little and open your eyes to the truth?'

Like frightened spiders, her eyes instantly scuttled away and hid in the dark network of wrinkles and moles. Pitiful, senile, unable to think of a single argument, she sat sighing while he explained to her in simple language the structure of the stars and the cause of lightning and thunder, which our barbarous ancestors ascribed to the Prophet Elijah whereas it is nothing but electricity crackling in the clouds.[1]

'Try to understand, Mama: there is no God,' he whispered to her mentally, doing his best to soften the blow by the subtle, inaudible method

_____

[1] 'What am I doing?' a doubt as brief and remote as a quiver of summer lightning went through his mind. He strolled about the darkening room, collecting his thoughts. 'No, it would be wrong,' he told himself as if taking a strong line with someone else. 'It's all very well attend-

of delivery. It was not an order he was giving her, not a stern decree to rid her mind of its rubbish—he merely conveyed to her, as simply as to a child, a breath of truth as gentle as a summer breeze.

The old woman took off her shawl and wiped her forehead.

'No, don't cry, Mama. Don't torture your poor weak heart,' he anaesthetised her silently. 'All is well. You feel a lightness, a sweetness you have never known before. You are at last free of the dark web of terrors they have been weaving round you ever since your childhood, my poor Mama. In a moment, your own aged lips will announce the blessed, liberating gospel: there is no God.'

'There is no God,' she articulated, her eyes bulging and her speech punctuated by pauses and gulps as if she were having hiccups. 'No God. No Prophet Elijah, they've shot him. It's all electricity. Thunder is electricity ... Have a little cheese and sour cream, Lenny love, you don't eat enough . . . There's no God. No angels in heaven. No cherubim. All gone ... Eat a little,

---

ing to the psychological needs of mankind—I can't neglect my lonely mother, caught in the trap of ancient superstition. It isn't easy, of course. It's hard, Comrades. But pulling down means pulling down, rescuing means rescuing, you have to go the whole hog.'

sonny, you have to keep up your strength. Look at you, you're as thin as a shadow . . . There's no God . . . What about it, love, just a tiny little bit of cottage cheese . . .'

So importunate was her pleading, so full of compassion for his gnarled and wasted flesh, that it suddenly occurred to him: if he were slowly and painfully putting his mother to death she would still remember to say with her dying breath: 'Do have a little cottage cheese, Lenny, please, love, it's good for you.' And when faith in God has been finally extinguished on earth to the last spark and the whole screaming mob of us is handed over into the power of Satan, this absurd maternal incantation will be all that's left to remind us of everything we have lost . . . 'Lost? Why lost? How?' He caught up with his thoughts. 'What is all this? Why the "screaming mob" and why Satan of all things? And what has cottage cheese to do with it?'

'There's no God,' the old woman mumbled slowly, monotonously, like a litany, her lips deathly pale. 'No God, no God,' she went on like a gramophone record, although Leonard—his thoughts having struck an obstacle and bounced off course—was no longer dictating to her.

'Strange, very strange,' he muttered, shaking his head. 'Very, very strange . . .'

'Comrade Makepeace,' Proferansov tottered out of the shadows. 'You won't mind if I go and

have a cigarette while you're talking ideology
with your Mama? It's after nine . . .'

It was true, the room was getting dark. Leonard bent over his mother and helped her to
come back to her senses. The old lady sighed,
blew her nose, shuffled her feet and called upon
the Saints, throwing off the effects of science and
resuming her normal, barbarous state of mind.
Looking hurt and moody, Makepeace hastily
instructed Proferansov to see her home, fix up
her sink, get her a couple of pails of water from
the well—as a special favour to him, Leonard—
and come back at the double because there was
still some work he wanted to do tonight. It was
all very urgent, he said, seeing his mother off,
picking up her things, fumbling and repeat-
ing himself, obviously distracted and out of
sorts.

'Shall I ask Serafima Petrovna to come in?'
Proferansov asked, unwilling to leave him alone
in this state. But Makepeace curtly refused,
adding that he would not be having supper with
his wife, he was too busy, would Proferansov tell
her.

It was dusk, the summer day was making its
leisurely way out, hesitating, stopping and coming back, forgetting and remembering things,
starting all over again to collect its belongings and
stumbling blindly into the furniture. On such
evenings skeins of thread and scraps of material
fly in armfuls about the house, making you sus-

pect that the air, empty by day, is inhabited by a shadowy fauna at night. 'There,' you say to yourself, as you notice the flick of a tail in the far corner of the ceiling and something swings down, grows to the size of a biggish infusorium and floats slowly across the room.

Sensitive people react strongly to such influences. Their ears buzz as if they were hearing lute strings, they feel a pricking in their thumbs and their fingers become faintly luminous from contact with invisible and unstable matter. But should we take this shimmer for the play of living creatures or imagine that we see in the wreathing dusk the reflections of astral bodies known to the profane as ghosts? Of course not! This would be contrary to all adult experience. What we mistake for ghosts are the evening shapes of the perfectly ordinary thoughts which all objects are constantly exchanging and which fill the room with their melancholy restlessness.

Oh the meditations and the monologues of inanimate objects! How comforting is their music! How often have they brought us safely to port amid the storms and agitations of life! Where should we be without the stream of consciousness which every object emits in its own specific and inimitable key and which enables us, as easily as though by magic, to establish its identity and function in life?

How otherwise could we tell the meaning of the

countless phenomena which assail our consciousness from all sides? We would be hopelessly lost
before we were even across the threshold. We
would mistake the sprawling armchair in the
middle of the room for a heap of rubble and
confuse it with the silhouettes of ruined
towers and pagodas trying, from outside the
window, to divert our attention to themselves.

But the armchair, deep under its faded and outmoded *drap-de-dame* upholstery, has a heart of
gold. Overflowing with tact and delicacy, its
whole being, from the top of its curved spine to
its curly feet, mutters, 'I am an armchair,' and
purrs and invites us to rest and relax in its cosy
lap and forget our cataclysmic preoccupations—
and we are drawn to it like a butterfly to a flower
and we go and sit in the armchair.

Whereas the ruin of the monastery is, by con-
trast, full of harsh inflammatory thoughts and
bears its mutilation with sullen endurance. It
shouts to us from the distance, 'Come, traveller,
sit beside me and meditate the riddle of the universe!'—and we go from the armchair to the ruin.

How is it then that man alone in his blindness
dares to shatter the harmony of being with his
irresponsible din? How dare he change the course
of mighty rivers or fell ancient trees nurtured for
a higher purpose than his? Mould and reshape
your minds as much as you will, turn yourselves
into cogs and wheels, the whole crazy mob of
you, for all I care! But keep your hands off trees

and stones! and old women—keep them off your wretched mothers—d'you hear me? don't you dare touch them . . .

'Who is there?' Makepeace looked over his shoulder.[1] 'Who is there?' he repeated slowly and distinctly, trying to sound calm, businesslike and stern.

The tomb-like silence in the room spoke of the presence of an authoritative guest, featureless though he might be and determined not to reveal himself in bodily form.

'Who goes there? Who are you? Speak! I order you . . . Please . . .'

Unwilling to have him on my hands in hysterics, I spoke in a low voice:

'I apologise for invading your privacy. But I have been following your career for some time, and I find that you abuse your power. Remember that it may be taken from you as suddenly as you received it. I don't as a rule interfere with people who are obsessed by an idea whether for good or evil. But in your case I am responsible, my dear

---

[1] Kochetov, still at his post, quickly stuffed his cap into his mouth for fear of betraying his presence by an inadvertent reply. But when, a moment later, he looked through the chink again, he was surprised to see Makepeace wandering like a ghost at the far end of the room and blindly, cautiously groping in the air which was filled with nothing but the floating shadows of dusk.

sir, because you only hold your so-called gift of magnetism as a temporary loan from me. My name is Proferansov—Samson Proferansov. You have already heard about me from an individual who bears my name and who chooses to regard himself as a distant relation of mine, though he has not the slightest grounds for this assumption. He will tell you a lot of cock-and-bull stories—what is important in them is not the alleged facts which your court historian borrows from rumours and anecdotes, but the general atmosphere created by my continued attachment to the earth which bears and buries us all. You will oblige me by not confusing me with vampires or the daemonic possession of hysterical women or any other offspring of an unquiet conscience. I . . .'

'Hands up!' he hissed, discharging all his will power, point blank, in the direction of my voice. 'Drop your weapons! Hands up! Confess: you are a spy in a special container, infiltrated by the Centre. Remove the invisibility device at once.'

His professionalism amused me—a skinny, snotty, cross-eyed brat who dreamed of an empire and was going round in circles, whistling in the dark and trying to see what is neither by day nor night susceptible of optical observation! I was strongly tempted to tweak his nose or bounce him against the ceiling but I regarded such practical jokes as in doubtful taste and had long since given them up. I merely advised him to beware of spies and agents who infiltrate the soul and destroy its silence by their furious clamour: compared to them, the honest snoopers who dog a man's footsteps or hide behind a curtain to listen to his conversations are humble supernumeraries who can only add a little spice to his situation but nothing to the abysmal depth of his vicissitudes. With this I tweaked the curtain in front of the half-open window, to let our silent witness know that his activities were not unobserved.[1]

'Avaunt! Avaunt! Vanish!' cried Makepeace in his extremity and hearing someone crash out of the window sank exhausted into an armchair, his heart hammering.

The torn curtain hung like a faded trophy. The full moon shed its desert light upon the empty

---

[1] Kochetov, unable in his terror to make out who was arguing with whom, thought at first that Makepeace was talking to himself in two different voices. Leonard looked as if he were weaving spells on the dark air mixed with the last afterglow of the sunset and the first frosting of moonlight which here and there added to the confusion. The money on the walls came briskly to life. The Celestial Emperors* pointed their sharp little muzzles and winked and nodded and rustled their greasy little beards in apparent

* Reference to the Oriental features of Lenin whose picture is on Soviet notes.

stage. But as it gradually took its place in the familiar setting of the room, the whole rumpus became understandable and natural—the result of insomnia, overwork, frayed nerves and a gust of wind stirring the curtain and slamming a shutter. The only thing that worried Leonard was the absurdity of the childish incantation which had escaped him in the excitement of the moment. Yet it was the worry that was absurd! He would have done better to smile and be grateful for the native muddle uppermost in his head, which had enabled him to decline the dangerous proximity of the one whose advent he was hastening . . .

Was the city of Lyubimov really to become the cradle of the Dragon? Was the mind of Russia, wound up like a spring, destined at some

---

solidarity with their owner who was spinning round and round the room faster and faster, goading himself on by his own shouts.

Kochetov's panic reached its climax when, by straining his ears, he caught the reference to his own part in the Saturnalia, and it was just at this moment that the curtain whipped out and grabbed him by the hair.

'Avaunt! Avaunt! Vanish!' came Leonard's strangled cry as from the distance of another world, and in implicit obedience to his command the agent went crashing to the bottom of the drainpipe.

appointed hour to fly off its spindle and send our little gilded orb flying with it to all the swinish devils of Hell? Or would a childish incantation, escaping us at the last moment, save us to the confusion of the enemy and the ruin of his plans? Or was it better for me, his kindly genius, to get away while the going was good, vanishing as discreetly as the daylight and leaving Makepeace in the belief that nothing had gone wrong which couldn't be put right after a good night's sleep?

'Cowards shouldn't play cards,' he muttered irrelevantly as he staggered out on to the balcony.

Light and emptiness were all around him. The faint pink haze of the afterglow was dissolving on the horizon, vanquished by the unalloyed, unmitigated brilliance of the moon which had entered upon its phase of maximum radiance. It dazzled his eyes. The wind syphoned steadily. The pale cosmic dust of clouds whistling past the moon gave it the appearance of an unmanned capsule sent into orbit and flying at its appointed speed.

'So does our little gilded orb speed into the future,' ran like a belated echo through his mind, immediately accompanied by the soft chords of a piano. Succumbing to the radiance, his lovely wife was playing a farewell overture before retiring for the night. He allowed her to continue. Returning to the H.Q., Proferansov found him in a state of illuminated exhaustion.

'There's still a drop of paraffin left—shall I light the oil lamp? Or perhaps the lamp of Ilyich as a special treat?'*

Makepeace remained silent and the old man dared not, without permission, waste the current from the accumulator which also served the border network (the power station had broken down).[1]

'Do you think it's true, Comrade Makepeace, that somewhere up there at the far end of the Constellation of Dogs a planet is already enjoying the future we are still so actively pursuing?'

Makepeace failed to react. Slumped against the door jamb, he was watching as though hypnotised the triumphant progress of the moon. The throbbing of the dark veins on his wasted forehead was the only sign that his soul had not departed his body.

Proferansov pulled him timidly by the sleeve:

'You wouldn't give me the order to go to bed, Comrade Commander?'

'Hullo, Savely! It's you, is it?' Lenny calmly turned to his secretary. 'I keep meaning to ask you more about that Proferansov you once told

---

[1] And we had not yet found a way of extracting paraffin from sunflower seeds.

* Ilyich: Lenin, who said that socialism plus electrification equalled communism.

129

me about—an ancestor of yours, I think you said, a learned gentleman . . . I'm sorry, I'm too distracted to do any more work. And my ears keep ringing . . . Get some pillows and an eiderdown and make up a bed on the floor. Let's spend the night together, friend Savely, and will you please tell me all you know about him? Perhaps your anecdotes will help to shorten my sleepless night.'

A smile appeared on his waxen face. Never had Proferansov seen so pale, so sour a smile on his face before. —But had he ever seen him smile? He wasn't sure.

'Why anecdotes? The facts of his life are perfectly well known to me. But I don't expect you'll believe me . . .'

The old man was dying to go to bed, but he was anxious to play his role as chief historian which in the daytime was all too often crowded out by his functions as secretary, adjutant, batman and messenger. They spread a featherbed on the glittering floor and Makepeace reclined on it without undressing, one eye on the window where the moon shone brighter than an electric bulb, the other on the eager face of Proferansov who sat in his underclothes, cross-legged on a cushion like a Vizier, smoking a cigarette while he collected his thoughts.[1]

---

[1] This was an exception. Comrade Makepeace never allowed me to smoke in his presence.

'You won't interrupt me, will you?' He gave a preliminary cough.

'Not a word,' Makepeace agreed with unusual mildness. 'You can tell me as many lies as you like: I need to know the truth.'

Chapter Five

The life of S.S. Proferansov in this World and the Next

'Once upon a time there was a nineteenth century nobleman who lived on his family estate, his name was Samson Samsonovich Proferansov. He was a great philanthropist, theosophist, Diogenes and bibliomaniac, and he carried out scientific experiments in the hope of finding that Philosopher's Stone which fools covet in order to make gold and wise men because they wish to discover the meaning—if any—of life. In his spare time he sat in his *drap-de-dame* upholstered armchair and read novels by Turgenev and Goncharov in the original Russian, or worked on his satirical treatise, "The Fate of Two-Legged Animals", or wrote in his diary, or corresponded with his friend Lavoisier, another outstanding philanthropist and eccentric, though of a lesser stature than our hero by reason of his senile addiction to gypsies and restaurants.

'Samson Samsonovich hated the noise and

bustle of the city and lived in seclusion with his German housekeeper and his beloved Russian nanny Arina Rodionovna.* Once, when he was no longer young, he paid court to the Governor's daughter, a fashionable beauty who at first encouraged him, only to run away with a handsome hussar on the eve of the wedding. After that, he devoted himself to science, allowing nothing to distract him from his research. If a curious neighbour called, he would receive him looking like a bear, unshaven, in his down-at-heel slippers and old army coat, and insist on shaking hands although his own were filthy up to the elbow with some newly discovered chemical substance. The caller, however disgusted, didn't like to refuse, and before he knew where he was, his shirt sleeves were hanging on him in ribbons. Or if it was a lady, he clawed her round the waist with the fingers he had just been using to dissect a tapeworm and when she ran squealing from the house he would step on her train and rip it off. Thus gradually he discouraged all his visitors.

'Like Tolstoy who was another of his friends and correspondents, he would sometimes take a simple country girl into his house, teach her a little grammar among other things and afterwards marry her off as his niece to some gentleman in Petersburg, thereby creating the cadres of the intelligentsia of the future. But he never

* Pushkin's nurse.

got into trouble for any of his peccadilloes because he was held in esteem by the Emperor himself. Indeed, the Tsar Nicholas I often urged him to move to our Northern Capital for good, and offered him a well-paid position as his Court Astrologer. Having crushed the Decembrists* he hoped by this means to stem the tide of popular vengeance which was rising throughout the country, but the incorruptible scientist remained adamant:

' "Nothing doing, Your Imperial Majesty," he said. "Tomorrow with a favourable wind I sail home to my Penates. It's my destiny to die on my own estate near the godforsaken city of Lyubimov which has yet to make its mark as you will see. As for Your Majesty and you, Gentlemen Commissars, Senators and Governors, you and your enticing daughters will all come to a sticky end," and he snapped his fingers with a loud noise as if cocking a gun.

'The courtiers didn't like it very much but they took it for a joke and smiled sourly, making allowance for the famous philanthropist's eccentricities. But the old gentleman must have had a good laugh to himself on that day in 1917 when he read in his newspaper that all that lot were up for trial . . .'

'What's that? Have a heart, Savely! How could he read it in his newspaper? How could

* Abortive uprising in December 1825, led by liberal members of the aristocracy.

he read a newspaper at all when he must have been dead?'

'Really, Comrade Makepeace, you did promise not to interrupt. Don't you think I realise that there are certain unusual features in Samson Samsonovich's life? Where was I . . . Now look what you've done . . . I've lost the thread . . .'

'All right, all right, I'll keep quiet. You were telling me what a good Bolshevik your Proferansov showed himself to be in his conversation with Nicholas I.'

'He certainly did not. I never said anything of the kind. Proferansov lived a perfectly blameless life, as quietly as Robinson Crusoe on his island. He never built a single barricade and the only drumming he ever did was on the window pane in his room where he sat looking out at the snow-covered bushes and trees in his garden (the windows were made of Bohemian glass which had been specially ordered from Dalmatia). This he did by the hour, observing the beauties of nature and pondering the mysteries of creation until his German housekeeper interrupted him by blowing and puffing outside his oak door and saying: "Dinner is served, Sir. Come and eat your food before it gets cold."

'But he was as bad as you are, Comrade Makepeace, when you won't take time off to eat like a human being. "How can I think about dinner, Glasha," he asked her bitterly, "when love has fled from the world and I can think about nothing except how to restore it to the human heart? This is the mystery I am pondering and you come and talk to me about vermicelli. Am I never to have any peace?" And as soon as he finished dinner he would go back to his tormenting thoughts and his drumming on the window, and so it went on until one day he said to his housekeeper:

' "Frossya," he said . . .'

'Wasn't her name Glasha?'

'Well, couldn't he have changed his housekeeper by then? Stop picking on me. "Frossya," he said, "I want you to pack a suitcase with my warm underclothes. Have it ready for me by tomorrow. I am sailing with a favourable wind to India."

'No sooner said than done. Casting his fortune upon the waters, Samson Samsonovich embarked on the Russian frigate *Vityaz* and set sail for India.

'India! How can we conceive the splendour of that dream of travellers throughout the ages. Not by thinking of the delicacy of our northern spring, nor of the high noon of our summer, nor yet of our golden autumn, rival though it may the palette of Titian or of Levitan.* Only our Russian winter can sufficiently embolden our imagination—our winter with its cold as savage as the heat of the tropics, with its lianas on the

* Russian painter (1860-1900) famous for his poetic interpretation of the Russian landscape.

136

window panes, its capricorns on the ice, and the magical crystallography of every one of the snowflakes God adorns it with and sends fluttering in the sky like miniature humming birds. You have only to take your skis into the forest and there, in the icy stillness under the palm trees you see elephants nestling in the snow drifts, and glittering bisons and tapirs, and snowy giraffes craning their necks from among the branches—you don't know if you are in Russia or in India and you say to yourself: the Lord must love our wretched country after all, to have clothed it in so much beauty.

'Four long years went by before Samson Samsonovich came sailing back to his native shores.

' "Still alive, old lady? Nice to see you!" he said kindly to his nurse Arina Rodionovna who was sitting thoughtfully by the gate with a sergeant major clutched in her arms.

' "Wake up, Mikheich, looks as if the Master is back," she said and, thrusting the drunken sergeant with his curly moustache into a snow drift, went to light the master's way with a lantern at the end of a pole.

'Proferansov locked himself in his study and spent a whole month copying the book which the atamans of India had given him. Then he took to his bed with malaria and never got up.

' "Let Lavoisier know, send a message to Tolstoy," he kept muttering while he was ill.

"We've made a grave miscalculation. The purpose of life is not . . . the purpose of life is . . ."—That was as far as he got. The most important part of the message remained untold.

'It's always the same. A man lives and plans and winks at himself conspiratorially as much as to say: "Hold on, Volodya, it won't be long now," but when it comes to explaining what the great mystery was about—there he lies, the mattress springs scraping the skin off his back, and he can't find the right words. And that's the end.

'But it wasn't the end of Samson Samsonovich. They put him in his coffin and they buried him according to the rites, but he was soon back. Whether it was that his explorer's soul, weary of travelling, couldn't resist the attraction of home or his mind was itching to round off its discovery —all I can tell you is that every evening, as soon as the family sat down to supper, there was Samson Samsonovich in his disembodied state, grumbling and shuffling up and down the gallery and afterwards scratching with his pen in his study. So familiar a figure did he become that they missed him if he ever happened to be late. They looked upon him as their mascot and as the guardian of the family traditions irretrievably lost in our wicked age.

'I suppose you'll want to know where all these relations had suddenly come from. Well, there is a legend that the Governor's daughter had dumped her anonymous brat on his door step and he had chivalrously covered up for her. But my own belief is that when he was on his death bed he at last married his beloved nurse and childhood companion Arina Rodionovna, which is why, as I told you, there is a good chance that both you and I may be descended from that ancient Russian philosophical stock.

'But to go back to our Penates, one evening the old couple were at home but, although it was past his usual hour, there was not a sign of Grandpapa. To pass the time while they waited anxiously, they recalled the good old days when their daughter Tanya was a little girl and afraid of the ghost, the silly child, thinking it would gobble her up! "Don't you know it's our Grandpapa, our guardian spirit," they used to tell her, "it would be a very bad omen for us if he ever lost his temper and decided to stay away." So they reminisced while they listened for the creak of the floorboards in the gallery, where no one except Grandpapa dared to walk nowadays, or went down to his study to see if the incombustible candle were alight in the empty room. But there was no light anywhere, and no sound except the ancient oak trees moaning in the park.

'So that night went by and another and a third and still there was nothing!

'Torn with anxiety for Tanya—there must surely be a member of the family who was in trouble—they rushed to Moscow where she was now living with her husband and children (she had made a good match immediately after leaving the Conservatoire) but to their amazement found upon arrival that there was nothing wrong there either—the children well, Tanya fat and cheerful and the marriage evidently not on the rocks: her husband was grinning from ear to ear.

' "Grandpapa must simply have decided to revisit India . . ."

'But the next day the estate agent galloped up by train and arrived, all sooty, to tell them that the very night after they went away their house had gone up in flames and burnt like a torch— "Lucky there was no one sleeping in it or they couldn't have been saved—you've escaped by a miracle!"

'The revolution had broken out and all that remained of the richest home farm in the district was a heap of rubble and a few wisps of smoke.

' "Now do you see," the mother said as she packed their suitcases for Paris. "It's just as I told you. Grandpapa stayed away those three nights because he knew there was trouble brewing, he smelt kerosene in the air, and he found this way of giving us a signal. We must be very grateful to our old friend. And now the house is in ashes, the master smoked out and the ghost banished for ever!"

'But in this the emigrants were mistaken. Their

house was indeed in ashes, but the ghost stayed on, he even enlarged the field of his activities.

'I heard this from a retired Chekist* I was having a drink with. One day, early in the NEP†, he had dropped into a teahouse with a bunch of Red Army men, to get warm and incidentally to write up his report on the illicit still they kept at the back.

'Suddenly he hears a squeak and a thump and a crackle in his ear, as if someone had blown into the receiver, and a voice saying:

' "Hullo, hullo, ring up Lavoisier, ask Trotsky —who will restore love to the human heart? Who will encompass the mysteries of creation at a glance?"

'The Chekist looks up and there, sitting at the back of the room, near the still, is an old man with an intellectual face, drinking tea, reading a newspaper and not saying a word.

'Well, by the time they thought of asking him for his documents he had got up, buttoned up his coat to the neck, jammed his cap on his head, let out a cloud of grey steam and vanished amidst the roar and stink of the bubbling samovars. All they found at the spot where he had taken off was an ancient copper coin with a two-headed eagle on it, and the evening edition of *Izvestia* fresh

* Chekist—member of the Cheka as the Security Service was called in the early years after the Revolution.

† NEP—New Economic Policy—a policy of economic relaxation introduced by Lenin in the last years of his life.

from the printers. But up on the ceiling were the damp tracks of invisible felt shoes making for the creaking ventilator in the corner, and a strange voice could be heard through the rumbling of the cauldron:

' "We've miscalculated again. But the city of Lyubimov will make its mark."

'They looked outside but there was not a soul—nothing but the stillness, the snow glittering in the moonlight, and the runners of a sledge whispering from the other end of the earth: "Hist-Chekist-Hist-Chekist." The cold was terrible.

'Incidentally, one winter that same Chekist was on guard duty in Lenin's house in Gorky and he could hear Ilyich just the other side of the wooden wall, having treatment and working on the draft of the First Five Year Plan. Every evening he wrote and he clicked the beads of his abacus until about one, then he tiptoed out—no hat, no coat, his hands in his pockets—and slipped into the yard for a breath of air. There he stood in the crackling frost, kneading the snow with his feet and looking around him, and if there was no one about, he threw back his head—the bald top shone in the moonlight . . .

'Thoughtfully, methodically, Lenin bayed at the moon—he bayed at the moon, our Ilyich, knowing that he was soon to die. Every moonlit night it was the same. He howled, and he stopped and listened, and he howled again until he began to feel chilly and turned and ran as fast as his legs would carry him, his green eyes flashing in the dark, back to his writing and his calculating and his planning of the path we were to follow in life. It was a long time before the light went out in his little room.

'You'll ask me what relevance this has to my story—it hasn't. Except that if even Lenin—if even Vladimir Ilyich could have his moods, then why not a fine Russian gentleman who had never done any harm to anyone and who had found a much safer way of reaching the ultimate heights? It's phenomenal, you know, how people who will believe any rubbish will yet refuse to look at the facts. Even you, Comrade Makepeace . . . And yet there are a few curious biographical details about you as well. Only tonight when you were so fascinated by the moon, I thought any minute you'd do a Lenin on me. —You! a saintly man, the greatest general we ever . . . I'm not boring you, am I ? . . . Damn me if he isn't asleep! And I wasn't half way through . . . Snoring! Worn out at his general's post! Look at him, the squint-eyed devil, God forgive me, fast asleep !

'Poor mutt! Thinks he knows everything. Just because he's inherited the family manuscript and learned the A.B.C. of the gentry, he thinks he's sitting pretty. Well, you aren't, my friend. Your influence is waning, I can feel it myself. We've yet to see which way the wheel of fortune will turn . . . What are you groaning for? Sleep, rest . . . You'll need your strength. Pray God your Mama will visit Father Ignatius and you'll get better, you'll recover your sanity. Because this is a spell, that's what it is, all of it. And already people in town are talking about you and your black magic, and very soon they'll be saying, all of them, "Let's have nothing to do with that Squint-Eye—who knows if we won't have to answer for him before a court martial."

'Move over, you big bully. Can't you keep your elbows to yourself even when you're asleep? Oh well, all right. I'll lie at your feet. Don't worry. I won't sell you down the river. I'm your watchman and your counsellor and your nanny. Arina Rodionovna. Ruslan and Lyudmila*. India. I still wish I could write your biography. But there's never any time. Stills. Samovars. Samson Samsonovich. Vladimir Ilyich. Russia. Go to sleep.'

* Epic poem by Pushkin.

Chapter Six

Knife Edge

~~~~~~

The pigeon wheeled and set course for Moscow. It had no need of a flight plan, the call of its native pigeon cote was in its blood and the foretaste of arrival heartened it, much as the conclusion of this tale (now within sight) heartens the author who busily unwinds the threads of the plot and makes for home as fast as the pigeon released from its basket.

Why then has a conflicting voice spoken in its breast? Why does it anxiously look back and wobble in mid-air as though faced with a new choice of direction? —Don't choose, don't hesitate! Remember, it's eternity that matters, not the miles, the hours, the days! Fly straight on! No? How often do we betray our purpose through miscalculation!

A moment's struggle and the bird turned back, its wings leaden but its zeal renewed. A bird, however, does not betray its innate principles with impunity. Losing height and steadiness, it looped like a hare through the streets of the unfamiliar town. It missed the belfry by inches, just cleared the network of cables on the roof of the H.Q. but—dazzled by the glass door of the balcony where outstretched hands were waiting to receive it—flew blindly into the wall and fell, a bloodstained heap of feathers at the feet of Makepeace.

'Felt like an outing, chum? Well, you won't again!' He bent over the corpse of the repatriate. 'A carrier—I thought as much! Well, let's see what our internal enemies were concocting.' Careful not to get the pigeon's blood on his hands, he extracted the tight little scroll from the metal container attached to its leg. On one side of the sheet was the address in block letters—ANATOLE SOFRONOV. P.O.B.IOOOI. MOSCOW —on the other the message which, for some reason, was in clear. Makepeace had no difficulty in deciphering the tight neat hand.

Dear Tolya,

This is your friend and former colleague, Vitaly Kochetov, writing to you from Lyubimov. Do you remember, Tolya, how we used to walk about the silent streets of Moscow, discussing the books we had read and pooling our information about the latest security techniques?* What children we were! It all seems like a dream! But in

* See *The Trial Begins* by Abram Tertz, New York, 1960.

our era, Tolya, dreams have a way of coming true. Do you remember the brain servicing apparatus we dreamed of—a device to photograph people's thoughts while they were still only in their minds? Well, listen to this: the device exists and it is even more technically perfect than it was in our Utopia! Instead of merely putting their thoughts down on film, it sets them on their proper course right from the start! What d'you think of that? I have now completed my reconnaissance and I realise that Makepeace has been slandered by envious bureaucrats and dogmatists, in fact it remains to be seen if a foreign agency was not mixed up in it as well. Having seen him with my own eyes, coping with American spies, ghosts in special containers and other survivals of the past, I have decided to stay on. My only trouble is, Tolya, that before I had sorted out my ideas, I foolishly jumped from his window and broke my radio set. So this despatch goes to you by a service pigeon. It's an experienced bird and has even crossed mountain ranges before now, so I have no doubt it will reach you. Tell the boss not to send the air force against Lyubimov, my suggestion was a mistake. So far from fighting Makepeace we ought to welcome his initiative and apply his educational methods on a mass scale—this is the task imposed upon us by the situation of today. You know me, Tolya! You know I'm not an abstractionist, I'm one of the boys, will you tell them up there? And tell Katya, my wife, that I'll be sending for her soon. Incidentally we were wrong about the Jews, Tolya, we underrated them, the Jews are human beings like ourselves, don't you think? Goodbye, Tolya, but not for long I hope. I believe that when things have settled down you too will join me, and we'll clink goblets of cut glass once again and drink to world peace!

*Your Vitya**

Leonard now regretted the death of the pigeon. Had it reached Moscow, this communication from an eyewitness who had seen the light might have gained us sympathy in progressive circles. But there was one advantage: the message told him of the arrival in the city of a genuine, reliable friend, such as he had increasingly felt in need of. The briefest contact with our healthy moral climate had evidently been enough to convince the sensitive spy of the rightness of our cause.

'Where are you, my unknown friend? Don't hide from me. Hear my voice, the anguished voice of loneliness, and come to me ! . . . Come, Vitya . . .'

As though in answer, he heard a distant

* Tolya and Vitya are diminutives of Anatole and Vitaly. Kochetov and Sofronov are the names of two reactionary Soviet writers.

mechanical throbbing in the sky. It soon turned into a sickening metallic screech, making the earth groan, the woods echo and the lopsided little houses on the hillslope jiggle as in a fit. Leonard ran for the market place but, stunned by the noise, fell on his back in the cobbled street a couple of yards short of it.

With a terrifying roar the plane dived out of the woods. Truth to tell, it was no miracle of up-to-date rocketry but merely an ordinary, run of the mill bomber which had survived from the days of Stalingrad; spreadeagled like a cat with its muzzle pointing and its ears flat back, it leaped through the air, waggling its body, wilful and unpredictable. Even one such beauty with its proper load would have been more than enough for our ancient timbers—and this was only the flag-ship, it was followed by a whole squadron! Evidently the order had gone out to leave nothing of the city of Lyubimov.

Lenny lay watching the enemy plane as it dived, making for his face. What could he do? His face, stretched on the cobbles, as wide as the market place, made an excellent target, and the pilot knew that it's as easy to hit a man when he is down as to set a wood ablaze with a fire-bomb. Of course! He knew, he saw that Lenny's hollow cheeks were no more fireproof than banks of brushwood, his lips, pimply with bog rash, powerless to resist the blow, his eyes— quick! a simile for human eyes armed with nothing but the despairing gaze they fix upon the steel monster falling, falling, nearer with every second, with every thousandth of a second . . .

Perhaps you'll ask me: who cares about similes at such a moment, and why go on when the facts are clear—why the clumsy camouflage of outmoded metaphors when anyone can see that the hero is *kaput*? Wouldn't it be better to write with the calm, civilised restraint of a Feuchtwanger or a Hemingway? 'The gunner pressed the lever. Full stop. Brains spattered on the cobbles. Full stop. Doing up his buttons, he heard the water flushing in the toilet . . .'

Wait a minute! If we had a single battery, a single ramshackle carbine, do you think we'd still be howling to heaven in our ungainly prose? But where's justice? They have everything— planes, press, radio, telephones, lunatic asylums— and what have we got? Nothing! Nothing except our naked imagination! Crushed and waiting for death, what should we do but fly in its face and poke it in its purring muzzle with the first great monster of a blood-curdling hyperbole that comes to hand?

However you'll have your battle scene in its naturalistic version—always keeping in mind that our Lenny had his head properly screwed on.

Imagine the plane going into a nose dive . . .[1]

---

[1] . . . and a stricken man lying on the ground.

Its speed is murderous . . .[2]

The pilot is surprised to see . . .[3]

. . . the savage beast approaching and ready to sink its claws . . .[4] like spears into the sky.

As if . . .[5]

. . . the roaring plane . . .[6]

'Go away, you filthy bitch or you'll get what's coming to you!'

When the plane had obediently zoomed up and wheeled away followed by the squadron, Makepeace felt as if he had burst every vein in his forehead, but he had just enough strength left to raise himself on one elbow and speed the enemy with a parting message. The planes flew on without a backward glance. Five miles from the city they bombed an open stretch of marsh,

---

[2] . . . its target the man's face. The man fixes it with a tense look.

[3] . . . instead of buildings grimacing with terror, nothing below him but wild woodland sweating here and there with swamps and meres. The reason is that in his mortal desperation, Lenny screws up his eyes and darts them straight at . . .

[4] . . . into his eyes. His eyes shoot up like giant trees and thrust their tops . . .

[5] . . . the earth itself were planted with spikes, as if it had reared itself up in its blind rage and were coming at . . .

[6] . . . screaming at it:

presumably mistaking its undulations for camou-
flaged arms' dumps and the banks of brushwood
for the bastions of the monastery.

Leonard would gladly have blown them all up
with their own bombs, but his thirst for revenge
was checked by his foresight as a strategist and
he confirmed the airmen in their illusion that the
city was destroyed and the flames—they had seen
them with their own eyes—were licking the
charred remains of the Lyubimov deviationists.
It was better for us in the given circumstances to
sham dead. We needed a breathing space to
recover and hit back in strength.

'Comrade Commander, I request permission to
put myself under your orders,' came in a soft
tenor from just overhead.

In spite of the cruel ache in his back, the Commander turned over on his other side. His eyes
fell on a pair of bark shoes and peasant puttees.
The puttees, however, had a neat military twist
and the shoes stood with their heels together and
their toes apart.

'I am Vitaly Kochetov, retired universal agent.
Please arrest me. The enemy learned our location
from my portable radio post. The political
responsibility for the air raid is mine.'

The youth was in rags but he was standing to
attention. The massive hands with their large
fingers were eloquent of the craftsman long
familiar with the locksmith's tools. The face was

open, the nose tip-tilted, the eyes steady. He was exactly as Leonard had pictured him.

'Well met, Vitya! Glad to know you!' He got up. 'Let's have a talk quickly, before they all come hopping round us like fleas. I've got a job for you, I want you to help me with a long range magnetic magnifier . . .'

'Excuse me, Commander,' the velvety tenor broke in. 'Oughtn't I to be punished first? I must answer for my mistakes. I am responsible . . .'

'You'll be responsible all right!' said Lenny, more and more delighted with his rare find. 'From now on, you are my friend and my Chief Deputy!' He walked up to the neophyte and kissed him plumb on his boyishly pouting lips.

For the second week running the woods were on fire. Incendiaries had been at work. The soil was boggy but a fire in a bog can be surprisingly difficult to cope with. You put it out in one place, it comes up in another. You wouldn't think it possible for anything to burn with so much water and rotting timber all around, but the smoke comes up from the rot itself. No one knows how the fire spreads. Perhaps it goes underground in one place and comes up in another. You never see it spread—only the smoke steals along the ground and after a few days of standing in it the trees have turned into ready-made firebrands.

Such fires are too slow and gradual to do much damage and experienced people say: 'Leave it alone, it will burn itself out by the time winter comes.' But meanwhile the air in the city has a tang of smoke and as you breathe it you feel a sweet, restless expectation in your heart. Though what is there for us to expect?

The signalling system kept breaking down. Every morning Leonard sent work parties to the outlying woods, to fight fires or mend cables or trace the cause of a new short circuit. One day two old men went out with such a party and failed to return: they had gone to join their relations abroad.

June was a rainy month and the fires died down. But the hidden enemy continued to do his work on the sly. The wind had only to rise for the strange bitter tang to be back in the air and sometimes flakes of soot were blown along the streets. Meanwhile the excessive rainfall was threatening the harvest.

Gales and thunderstorms interfered with production on the farms. In one a bull was killed by lightning. The women in the fields were drenched by the downpour and terrified by the huge arrows streaking the black sky. A village girl had a miscarriage caused by a thunderbolt; the baby was the size of a kitten but had a beard and a moustache and a well developed male organ—lucky it was stillborn and could be shovelled out of sight! Envoys from the villages came foot-slogging to town.

'What can I do for you? Would you like a lightning conductor?' Leonard offered them the wonders of science. But the peasants milled about in the yard, grumbling and looking sly. No, they said, a lightning conductor was nothing, they could put one up for themselves. But what about putting a spell on the weather to regulate the rainfall? And when he reminded them that spells and miracles had long since been abolished by science, they all, with one accord, referred him to Father Ignatius, a remarkable priest, they claimed, who lived about fifty miles away, just past Wet Hill, and who had only to hold a service for the sun or rain to be turned on according to need. On one occasion the delegates scratched their heads and actually hinted that if Leonard couldn't work his magic any more, then what the hell was the use of him? And someone laughed . . .

Leonard straightened out their minds and stifled the voices of subversion on the spot, but he faced the facts: evidently the ship of state had sprung a leak. It was hard to know exactly why. Had he perhaps overstrained himself in his battle with the air force? or had the rot set in even earlier?

Who can tell the root cause of the decay of dynasties? When did the sunset over Europe or the decline of Rome really begin? Perhaps in the very noonday of its power, at the very zenith of a country's glory, some bored, farsighted genius is already quietly slipping away from its shores. Or perhaps at its very birth, long before it has developed its industries or put up its architectural monuments, a secretly minuted resolution has already doomed it to be swept away within X hours by another power, itself destined in its turn to come to an equally sticky end. Here we sit, you and I, wagging our tongues and scratching our heels, and who knows if there, outside the window, Ancient Rome isn't crumbling for unstated reasons at this very moment or, worse still, the whole world is coming to an end, and, as Sergey Essenin said, it's time to pack up . . .

Leonard vanished for days on end, working on the economic front or watching over law and order in the city. In gloomy solitude he patrolled the streets, gaunt and hollow-eyed, the dark veins knotted on his brow like a sheaf of forked lightning. He took to going about incognito. Disguised as some harmless character such as an accountant or a village foreman, he would drop into a pub crowded with people drawing their daily ration of vodka. (Ever since the death of the drunken jail-bird, consumption had been strictly limited to 150 grams a head. Not even Makepeace ventured to introduce total prohibition in a Russian city: try it and you'll get a revolution at once.)

'Tell me, what d'you think of our foreign policy?' he asked a legless war veteran who had put away his legal portion and was addressing himself to one obtained on a stolen coupon.

'What's there to think about it, chum? It's straight and just. It's a peace-loving policy as you might say . . . Cheers!' He drained his glass and smacked his lips. 'Our only trouble is this substitute vodka they give us as you know.'

'What d'you mean—substitute?' Lenny was staggered by the brazen insolence of the man. After his double portion he was red in the face and sweating like a pig, his eyes glazed and his speech slurred—what more did he want? But although he could hardly get his tongue round the words, he went on insisting that the vodka was a substitute, produced out of plain water by hypnosis.

'But how could you know such a thing even if it were true? Look at you at this very moment—you're drunk! Don't you feel drunk? Don't you experience all the pleasure of being drunk?'

'I do now, but judge for yourself—you could drink this Fascist brew all day and never get a hangover! Call that vodka?'

The cripple gave a sob and genuine drunken tears poured and dripped on to his greasy tunic.

'Cheer up, old man, don't take it so much to heart,' Leonard tried to comfort him.

'How can I help it? Do you realise?' he lowered his voice to a whisper. 'Do you realise that we've got a magician for our Tsar and a Jewess for our Tsarina?'

That evening Leonard had an explanation with his wife. He casually raised the question of her nationality when he dropped in to kiss her good-night.

'Not now, darling, I've got to work. Really, there's something almost Spanish about you . . .'

'I'm Russian according to my passport,' she readily explained. 'So was my mother. But my father was half-Greek half-Jew.'

'A *Jew*? With a name like Kozlov?'

'That was my first husband . . . My maiden name was Fischer.'

'Your *husband*? You've been married before and this is the first I hear of it! Would you mind telling me if you also had children?'

'Why "had"? I *have*—a little girl in Leningrad, she's with my in-laws . . . They took her over after the divorce. Oh darling! Don't look at me like that! I never meant to hide anything, but you never asked! Believe me . . .' He couldn't;— his faith was shattered, like the scent bottle he had sent flying with everything else off her dressing table and which lay in shivers on the floor, filling the room with its cloying smell. It was then, as she was picking up her belongings, that the woman unexpectedly snapped:

'It's all your fault! How much have I seen of you since our wedding? A nice honeymoon I've had ! . . .'

Suddenly, the Serafima he had once known popped from out her Dresden shepherdess disguise, measured him with an annihilating glance and popped back. It was over in an instant—the eyelids snapped open and shut, the cheeks flushed and paled, the grinning mouth tied itself in a bow.

'I'm sorry, darling, I'm sorry, forgive me, I love you, how could I . . .' she droned in a slow drugged voice.

He slammed the door, leaving the puppet to sort out its own feelings. Back in his room he hastily changed and washed. He couldn't rid himself of the impure and cloying smell of scent.

From then on, Serafima could no longer complain of her husband not giving her enough of his time. For hours on end he would pace to and fro like a caged wolf in front of the low divan on which she sat curled up, creasing her forehead and wringing her memory.

'Then there was the manager of the club. He was called Leonard, darling, like you. A very cultured and original man. With a tremendous sense of humour. We both adored Handel. His parting present to me was a book of Japanese verse, he dedicated it to me on the fly leaf: "Serafima, you are my Hiroshima, my all which I have lost." *Lost*, please note, darling. Then for about six months there was a terribly jealous Armenian, Tevosian, he was even more jealous than you are. A sailor, body and soul. One day he met me walking arm in arm with Issya and he nearly sliced the poor boy in half with his cutlass. Issya doesn't really count. He was just a boy. A strongly marked semitic type. A weedy youth. A pallid blossom from the pages of Novalis. But it's funny, you know, how tough some of these delicate blossoms are. Perhaps I'd better not tell you. I don't want to upset you again. Though goodness knows . . .'

'Don't you dare to keep anything back,' Leonard spat at her, scurrying past the sofa, and she continued to reel off her story with the perfect accuracy of an automaton.

'We once spent a weekend at a cottage near Ozerki. It had a wonderful view of the lake but we never got up to look at it. Issya kept biscuits and strong meat broth by the side of our camp bed. I don't think I've ever come across anyone so considerate. Except perhaps Almazov—I met him in the train on my way here, we shared the sleeper*. There was plenty of life in the old gentleman still. I used to call him *mon colonel*, though actually there was hardly anything between us, it was almost a platonic affair, more fleeting even than with Linde. Can you imagine, my sweet, I was so bored until I met you that I even flirted a little with our good doctor! Though only twice . . .'

'Shut up! Forget it.' Leonard could bear no more of it. 'Forget the lot of them, do you hear

* Men and women sometimes share the wagons-lit on Russian trains.

160

me? I'm the only husband you've ever had. Your bourgeois past is dead and buried, you've finished with it for ever.'

But on the following day, when she had obediently forgotten and was as innocent of her past as a child of six, he again ordered her to remember, to supply an additional detail on this, an explanation of that.

'Who else did you mess about with before that Genghis Khan of yours?'

'What Genghis Khan?'

'That Armenian, the one who nearly slit the other fellow's throat . . . And another thing— did you sleep with Handel or didn't you? Stop hedging now. Did you or didn't you? What are you laughing at? I'll teach you to laugh!'

In fact his wife was not as depraved as he chose to imagine. From the purest of motives, doing her best to please him, she had searched her memory for every scrap of evidence to prove to him that she was holding nothing back—and let's face it: what attractive and cultivated woman living in the thick of progress, couldn't, if she really put her mind to it, make a respectable build-up of her past? We all want the women in our lives to remain pure and unsullied but they don't always manage it . . .

Makepeace, of all people, should have known that he was playing with fire, that the more he fed his jealousy as a man, the more he consumed himself as a public figure and a statesman, yet he continued mercilessly to explore her heart—such is the insolent daring of the investigator, whether of cells or atoms, or of the deep sources of love in a woman's soul, and so true is it that man is incapable by his very structure of stopping on the way to knowledge and of checking his jealous intellect: the more you give it, the more it asks.

Devoured by his scientific curiosity, Lenny from time to time interrupted his blockade of the woman's mind in order to observe it in its natural habitat. With bated breath, shocked and fascinated, he watched the old, inaccessible image of Serafima Petrovna coming to life in the body of the puppet. Her movements coarsened. Idle and slovenly, she slouched about the rooms, shedding her belongings and treating the house with the carelessness of a billeted soldier. She swore and shouted at him, as if it were she who was head of the household:

'My stockings! They're on the piano. The piano, I said—are you deaf?'

And she meddled in politics.

Trying to distract her, he had himself in the old days put her at the head of the Ministry of Culture. Now she seized upon public education and immediately tried to enlarge the curriculum in order to include Feuchtwanger's *Ugly Duchess* and *Jew Süss* and Hemingway's *The Sun Also Rises* among the set books for the senior forms.

Without using hypnotic pressure—merely

by the force of logic and with the help of illustrations from life—Lenny argued the impossibility
of including both novelists: it would mean the
co-existence of two ideologies. What would be
the reactions of Mao-Tse-Tung or Palmiro
Togliatti to the news of the peaceful co-existence
of Hemingway and Feuchtwanger, side by side
and never even scrabbling on the library shelves
of the high school of Lyubimov?

'A lot you know about Western culture,' she
retorted. 'Anyway, did you give me Lyubimov
as a present or didn't you? Who is the owner?
Who is the queen here, you or I?'

How he loved her at such moments! How he
thirsted for the love, the sympathy, the admiration
of this lovely, arrogant woman, so different from
the one whose meek and unfailing devotion was
boring him to death! To get the most out of the
situation while achieving some sort of synthesis
in the end, he flung it in her face that she couldn't
be much of a queen if, at the crook of his finger,
he could make her cringe and crawl to him like
the meanest of trash. Thus he teased her into a
fury until she flew at him, spitting and scratching,
in all the splendour of her savagery. Then and
only then did he switch on the current, and the
woman, taken unawares, spun like a top and
collapsed, felled by a sudden humiliating access
of passion, while Leonard—as remote and
inaccessible as an idol—sat motionless, keeping
her at bay.

He did, however, get a surprise now and then and the longer the investigation continued the less did it go according to plan. More and more often, after collapsing on the floor, Serafima went into convulsions and raved and complained like a woman possessed:

'Ai ai kiss me cross-eyed devil pity puny starveling burning sweet to give birth to whelps with Feuchtwanger tusks tanks coming crush bite tanks coming run come away to Leningrad.'

Frantically switching the current on and off, he found that it no longer made the slightest difference to her state. Someone else had evidently tuned in on his wavelength and taken over the control of her shattered nerves. To preserve her sanity, he put her into a hypnotic sleep—this he could still do; she came round from it refreshed, and all was well for a couple of days, until the same quiet domestic hell broke loose again.

Lenny's only remaining comfort was his faithful friend and assistant Vitya Kochetov. A corner had been found for him in the basement—something between a monastic cell and a lumber-room —and there, after clearing it of its rubbish, Vitya had set up his technical plant. Lenny's heart lifted every time he entered the workshop. Tidily put away on benches and shelves or hanging on hooks on the walls, were wheel-rims, drills, gimlets, hammers, plasticates, acids and all the equipment for galvanising and soldering, while tucked away in a corner were small gauge vices and a compact anvil. As soon as Lenny set eyes on them, his fingers itched for the feel of a hammer or a rasp or a file.

There, at whatever hour he chose to drop in, he was sure of finding his friend at work by the glimmering light of the oil lamp. Vitya never chattered, never asked importunate questions and only occasionally whistled the waltz tune from the film *The Childhood of Maxim Gorky*. But if you said to him: 'Vitya, the bolt!'—with a single turn of the screw Vitya would settle the hash of the recalcitrant bolt, or: 'Vitya, the bung!'—Vitya took hold of the bung and a drill and drilled until the wind whistled through the bung. Thus in no time at all the two friends would turn out a bicycle anyone could be proud of.

Lenny was an old hand at the mechanics of transmission, while Vitya's field was electricity and calorifics: it was at his suggestion that the motor at the power station was mended, and he too initiated the research which resulted in our discovery of a substitute for petrol. (The motor wouldn't work without liquid fuel. By force of circumstances we learned to make fuel out of vegetable oils.)

Only the work on the magnifier was behind schedule. We were starting from scratch, of course—no arithmometers, no condensators—

and the obstacles put up by the opposition alone were enormous: we were persecuted by our enemies and let down by our friends.

One day, just after Makepeace had set out on his bicycle to see to the harvest, the mistress of the house came into the workshop.

'No, thank you, I've had it,' Vitya politely refused her invitation to lunch and, hastily fitting a whetstone to a vice, assumed an expression conveying: 'I'm terribly sorry but this urgent problem prevents me from taking advantage of your kind hospitality.' He dared not look her in the face for fear of the dazzling smile which, he knew, was saying as always: 'If you think you can get away from me, my lad, you've got another think coming.'

'Is it true, Vitya, that you took part in disarming Berya's gang?' She smoothed her hair with a gesture perfectly calculated to chill any man's spine. 'No . . . don't tell me . . . I was forgetting the penalties agents are made to pay for their indiscretions . . . You know, I once thought of being a spy myself. It's so fascinating! The dangerous contacts, the secret rendez-vous . . . Think of the tragedy of a woman drinking champagne with some foreign diplomat at the risk of her life—he doesn't appeal to her as a man, but duty is duty, and she cheerfully offers him her youthful body . . .'

'I don't know what you're hinting at,' Vitya blushed. 'As you know, I've retired. I never cared for the job.'

Glancing round, he caught sight of her kneecap: it showed modestly enough through her negligée, but somehow in so pointed a manner that he couldn't bear it and looked away.

'What's the use of pretending, Vitya? —Do leave your lathe alone for a moment! —I won't give you away. Don't you realise that I'm as much his prisoner as you are yourself? Stop thinking of me as his wife. What kind of a husband is he to me? I've never even slept with him ! . . . Let's run away! I'll help you to steal the plans he keeps in his safe. Without them he will be helpless. He's lost his power over us as it is. I am completely in your power, Vitya—do you know that?'

His athletic torso was bathed in sweat. The red-hot metal stung his skin. The file sang and wailed like a violin under his fingers, but not loudly enough to drown her voice.

'Once we are in Leningrad, we'll use his plans . . . We'll raise our own standard. We'll lead an army against Lyubimov . . . I'll bear you a son, Vitya. You'll be my favourite, my prince consort, my deputy king . . . Believe me, Mao-Tse-Tung will offer us his hand in friendship. At the worst we'll give up Central Asia for a time. We'll sacrifice the Caucasus. We'll spread the conflagration to Europe. I'm serious, Vitya!

It's not some petty little provincial centre I've got in mind. I promise you . . .'

What wouldn't a spoiled, ambitious woman promise in such a case? But what future did her promises hold out for Russia? Chaos, sheer chaos. Anarchy and civil war. Roads ambushed, trains derailed. Black banners, pink negligées. *Trains baring their knees and skidding off the rails.* Kneecaps, cogs, cops . . . Bet she's got buffers under her skirt, frills and buffers . . . *Trains with thundering buffers skidding off the rails.* That file is overheating. Red flames, black trousers. I'll never give up the Caucasus. Favourite of all the Europes. Anarchy, sheer anarchy. In frills, *in trains skidding off the rails* . . . No, you don't, damn you!

File tilted, shoulders squared, lips as firm as pliers: 'Don't come nearer, lady, or I might kill you. For Russia, for Lyubimov, for Lenny, I wouldn't spare my life!'

For a long time afterwards Vitya whistled the waltz tune, considering whether to say anything to the Chief or not. In the end he decided not to. The Chief had enough on his plate. He had indeed.

Lenny's strength was failing by the day and by the hour and he hardly ever now made use of magnetism: he mainly relied on pep-talks. When I finally called on him to tender my own resignation on grounds of old age, he didn't even argue, he only asked reproachfully:

'Ratting, Savely Kuzmich? Going the same way as the others?'

'Not at all.' I went up to the desk on which the district map was lying open. 'It's just that it's time I stayed quietly at home and got on with my chronicle of your achievements—I won't get far with them sitting here, Lenny, looking at the signalling lights. And then I've got to do some gardening, it's just the season, the carrots need weeding, and people are so dishonest nowadays, you wouldn't believe it, yesterday they pinched that gosling you allowed me to keep. So now I'll get down to our book, Lenny, I've been thinking about it all along—just as you told me to . . .'

'You're very smart all of a sudden,' he gave me a disapproving look. 'Collar, tie, cufflinks, a proper *stilyaga*.* Is that for going abroad? You missed your chance last night, a whole bunch of defectors left.'

'I'm going to write, I tell you. Would I defect from my subject? You ought really to raise my pay, Lenny, now I'm joining the ranks of creative artists!'

He hung his head—thinking, I suppose, about rates of pay and rations and the trouble with the harvest. Then he asked me half-heartedly about

*Intellectual Teddyboys who imitate the Western style of dress.

the style in which I was writing my book. It was then I presented him with the bouquet I had kept for just such an occasion. Whipping it from behind my back and putting it in a prominent place, I adjusted my tie and my cufflinks and delivered myself of the following monologue:

'How beautiful it is! How fresh! How full of all the tints and scents of nature—this bouquet composed of the wild flowers which grow in such abundance in our humid soil. Note the cunning, the elegance, the artistry of its arrangement. See how the lanky trefoil sets off the fleshy juiciness of the hollyhock and how the wanton buttercup flirts with the timid daisy. Let our style be similar to this. Like blossoms in a bouquet, let the words dazzle the reader's eye and babble, each its tune, the cornflower laughing, the crimson clover proudly holding up its pompous head, while the jasmin drips its languid, pale and esoteric charm. Let all be free to nod and sway on their slender stems, panting and frolicking in unison, while competing in the beauty, artistry and finish of their petals, bells, cockscombs and festoons. For such is the luxuriance of style to which our native taste responds and which befits the greatness of our city, its colourful history and its new achievements under its brilliant leader.'

'That'll do,' said Lenny, so impressed that he was blowing his nose. 'You've certainly got a colourful style. But what you lack, Proferansov, is clarity of mind and simplicity of heart. That's a serious artistic failing, Proferansov. Your style is mannered and your words are full of quibbles. Altogether you are a tricky customer, a slippery futurist. Are you playing the fool deliberately, I wonder? Are you still bursting with spite from your unregenerate days?'

On and on he went, criticising my art. I preferred not to argue with him about why or where there was a certain morbidity or *schadenfreude* concealed in it, but I did show him that at least I had kept a conscience and a sense of shame.

'Don't you see,' I said, unconsciously adopting an affected pose, 'don't you see that I'm a bashful maiden who defends her virtue?' And I reminded him—still, for some reason, keeping the pose— of all the tricks our women had had recourse to in order to outwit the Fascist rapists—of how they soiled their skins with mud and cow-dung and sat, crawling with lice and drooling in their filth, waiting for the victorious return of their red-starred bridegrooms. There have been many such examples . . . Similarly, throughout our history our gifted men have passed for fools and our honest men for scoundrels—simply because our conscience warns us that it is not becoming for a man to bare his soul unless he has first coated it with filth. Thus a man will often swear or lie, or steal, or give his neighbour's wife a tumble in the hayloft, for no reason other than to preserve his soul in its protective cuirass, like a jewel in its casket, safe under lock and key . . .

'By the way, you don't happen to have come across the book I keep in my safe?' Leonard asked me, obsessed with his own troubles. 'You know the one . . . that old book in a thick leather binding.'

It turned out that he had kept the book under lock and seal in a metal container in his study and had worn the key on a chain in place of a cross. After he had learned it by heart, he had never bothered to look at the text again as long as he was confident in himself and happy about things in general. But recently he had felt the need to refresh his memory of one particular passage, and had found the container empty although the locks were intact and the seals unbroken. It came to me in a flash—who could have requisitioned the book other than Samson Samsonovich, the deceased gentleman who had lent it to us as a favour for a time and had now recovered his property?

'More of your fairy tales,' Lenny shrugged wearily and, after a brief silence, asked me if I remembered where, exactly—in which pool in our shallow river—we had sunk the weapons of the militiamen. I froze. So it had come to that! After all our fine speeches. Now it was goodbye to brainwork! All I said aloud were a few parting words of comfort:

'Don't worry, Chief. It didn't all go into the

river. Have a look in the cottages and you'll find a couple of dozen rifles . . . Look, it's clearing. God willing, the clouds will blow away and we'll save the harvest. All we've got to do is hold out until the cold weather—after that no one can get at us through the woods. Cheer up, Lenny, we'll hold out . . .'

But my soul inside its protective cuirass was whining: 'We can't! We won't!'

So deep in thought after his parting with Make-peace that he hardly knew where he was going, Proferansov left behind him the city gates and the fenced suburban gardens, and found himself in front of an outlying cottage; it nestled in a clump of willows on the muddy bank of the narrow river. The cooling sun was gently rock-ing on the dark and scummy waves—it was close on six. Clouds of mosquitoes hung in the air and a sour tang of smoke drifted from the woods. A pockmarked young woman was rinsing her washing in the stream and Proferansov asked her if he could see her companion. It was to this retreat that Tishchenko had withdrawn after his fall from power, to rest from the cares of office and devote himself to fishing. Shielding her eyes with her soapy hand, the girl yelled in a barbarous dialect:

'Semyon! Where are you, you old devil! Someone to see you.'

'Here!' came from the reeds along the bank.

'How do you do, Semyon Gavrilovich,' Proferansov bowed and seated himself on an up-turned pail.

Absorbed in the contemplation of his float, Tishchenko said 'Hullo' without turning his head.

They sat in silence. After a while they lit cigarettes. Passing his home-grown tobacco to his host, Proferansov commiserated:

'What an out-of-the-way place they've banished you to, Comrade Tishchenko, those wretched deviationists.'

'No one's banished me,' said the former Secretary. 'I moved because I chose to. The air is healthy and the fishing's good. Well, what news?'

'Am I the first?' the old man jiggled excitedly. 'You'll remember, won't you, Comrade Tishchenko—I wanted to be the first to assure you of my continued loyalty and to tell you that we won't put up . . .'

'Well—not, so to say, the first . . . Dr Linde rolled up the other day, also claiming he was a victim . . . What's eating him, do you know?'

Proferansov laughed and told the news of the trouble in which our court physician had landed himself. As soon as Makepeace learned of his last year's affair with Serafima Petrovna, he had demoted him from the rank of Chief Medical Officer to that of hospital orderly.

Savely was the more amused because not even

he, who had been Linde's closest friend and confidant, had heard of his adventure until now, so discreet had the doctor been. Another piece of gossip he had nosed out was that the First Lady had recently turned up on Linde's doorstep in the middle of the night and tried to get him to run away with her, but Linde had stuck his whiskered face out of the window and hissed:

'You must be out of your mind, Citizeness! I'm not your lover and never was.'

Tishchenko sighed and spat thoughtfully into the river.

'She used to be quite a girl.'

'How can you say that, Semyon Gavrilovich! A skinny hag! I must say I prefer them with a little fat on their bones . . . So you won't forget that I'm a victim too. Makepeace has dismissed me on account of my convictions. Once you're back at the helm . . .'

'Helm?' A shadow of displeasure veiled the banished ruler's phlegmatic glance. 'I'm very happy where I am. Soon I'll qualify for my pension, I'll sit on the bank and watch . . . You know what, old boy, they're beginning to rise. Take my spare rod if you like, but keep out of my way.'

Proferansov took the rod and moved obediently a few paces away. He sat watching the slow, scummy waves and waiting for a bite. He was warmed by the sun and cooled by the breeze. Occasionally a mosquito stung him and now and then he had a catch. The weather in Lyubimov had returned to normal.

We never discovered who it was that Serafima Petrovna left with in the end. More than twenty people went on the same day, among them the headmaster of the school, who took the school horse and buggy. Makepeace also discovered defalcations at the H.Q.—the wallpaper had been damaged with the help of hairpins, a flat-iron and a razor. In the general commotion the fugitive had got away with some 5,000 roubles—where would she get value for her tattered notes?

Leonard made no attempt at pursuit. With the dazed indifference of the shipwrecked he walked the familiar streets, seeing everywhere the traces of his unfulfilled dreams. Here was the site of the Stadium—one ditch had been dug and half the monastery wall demolished for bricks; over there were the foundations of the Matrimonial Palace with its Fountain of Love, planned in honour of the traitor and embezzler of today; and further along the Avenue, still hidden by the mists of the future, were the projected Palaces of Science, Youth, Labour, Realistic Art, and a small and unassuming Palace of Bicycle Production and Repairs.

Among these unfinished monuments and unplanted gardens, children were playing in the dust and rubble, while a peasant, calm and morose, pissed unashamedly into a concrete mixer half full of cement. No one stopped him, and the Generalissimo himself merely averted his face.

Drunkards were lying about here and there among the excavations in the principal avenue. They were not, alas, overcome by hypnosis but by the rot-gut brandy which again was being illicitly distilled. No one picked them up, no one moved them out of Leonard's way. People gathered idly in the streets, talked, laughed, brawled, played dice or hopscotch, and melted away at the sight of Makepeace. They were a little afraid of him. As he passed a tumbledown fence, he heard an angry woman threatening her child:

'Just you wait, Cross-Eye will come and turn you into sausage meat.'

What had he done to them? What had they against him? Hadn't he given up his life to them, crippled his health in the service of the savage brutes who, the moment his energy began to fail, came at him with jeers and insults? For their good and with their consent he had taught them discipline, rid them of their vices and hardened them through work. Of their own will they had taken part in the requisitioning campaigns which he had conducted so humanely that the individual always had a little something left against a rainy day. Hadn't this very hag, who was now teaching her brat to distrust the authorities, begged him to take her poultry, raving like a schoolgirl about

cultivating her mind and driving a tractor—
though no doubt a broomstick would have suited
her better!

A terrified clucking made him stop and turn.
A hen was fleeing in panic down the Avenue,
pursued by the elderly party he had that very
moment had in mind. Her skirts hitched up, the
old woman was astride a broomstick, but this
didn't prevent her from covering the ground
so fast that it seemed as if at any instant she
might become airborne.

'Will she really?' he had time to wonder
anxiously before she pushed the ground away
from her with her stick and soared half a dozen
yards into the air. With a flash of bare heels and
thighs, she came smack down on the thatched
roof of a low barn and, pausing only to draw
breath, poured a stream of abuse upon the hen.

'Damn fool of a woman! Now she'll draw a
crowd!' No sooner had this occurred to him
than curious onlookers came running from every
side. 'Disgraceful!' he thought indignantly,
watching the mob and as yet unaware that the
growing epidemic of disorder was purely the
result of the chaos in his own mind.

He had yet to realise that in this dying hour of
his power and glory, his gift of suggestion
had been restored to him a hundredfold. Never
as now had he been able to sway the multitude
and bring its strength and energy to the boil.
Only his own intentions was he unable to control

—and every whim and rubbishy notion that went through his mind was instantly transmitted to those around him and accepted as a command.

How can any man be sufficiently master of his soul to know and to check every twist of his perpetually seething imagination in advance? 'Don't panic!' he tells the crowd, and it obeys him. But in that same moment a hulking brute of a fellow strikes him by his resemblance to a bull. Immediately the brute paws the ground, bellows and rushes at the bystanders, who calmly allow themselves to be gored (haven't they just been told that they mustn't panic?) thereby further confusing and complicating the situation.

Loyally and efficiently, the people of Lyubimov applied themselves to their set tasks, including those which Leonard was utterly unconscious of having set them. Women took off their clothes. Men divided into teams and fought each other grimly, without unnecessary noise, with all the resolution they could bring to a collective undertaking. Children below the age of reason imitated the domestic animals, while the animals joined the mêlée in their own shape and contributed their share to the confused effect of the alliance between autocracy and popular freedom.

Hens crowed, goats barked, a cow miaowed and jumped over a fence. The lout who thought he was a bull rushed at his girl friend.

'Drop dead, damn you!' All Makepeace intended was to check the sensualist who was clearly lost to shame, but the youth roared, fixed him with a look of burning hatred and dropped dead of a heart attack.

Trying to control the more consistently violent of his subjects by inducing in them a temporary loss of consciousness, he found himself again and again giving the order 'Die!' instead of 'Sleep!'—so when he did, the sleepers never woke up.

With a violent effort he succeeded for a brief moment in immobilising the crowd—everyone froze in his or her attitude of demented aggression or depravity. But the sight of the forest of up-thrust and contorted limbs broke his nerve. 'Look at that old man, grinning like a dog, now he'll start to yap,' an insidious voice whispered in his ear—and the man yapped and the scene exploded into renewed violence.

Beware of distractions . . . Learn to think with care, straight along the taut line stretching back from the desired goal, a line as swift, as pure and as unwavering as an arrow—think straight . . . Don't waste yourself on trifles . . . Don't pollute the air with nonsensical notions . . . You can never tell the result . . .

His back against the thatched barn, Makepeace was afraid to move: a single unconsidered word or gesture and the whole city might uproot itself and go leapfrogging off into the woods and bogs. But events were now following their course without his assistance. Already the messenger on the broomstick, who had opened the proceedings and had since familiarised herself with her job, had swept across the sky. Planing and whirling like a windmill above the roof tops, she delivered her absurd oration:

'Ai ai cross-eyed devil pity puny starveling burning sweet to give birth to whelps with Feuchtwanger tusks tanks coming crush bite tanks coming run come away to Leningrad!'

With this she vanished, and immediately the tension relaxed, the excitement died down. The women hastily snatched up their clothes and fled. Their voices could be heard from their back gardens, calling their children home. The men wiped the blood off their faces, rounded up the cattle and collected the dead. They were hoarse and sullen as after a heavy drinking bout. But had they taken in the meaning of what they had been through and what was happening to them? Leonard, for one, had not.

'Stop! What's the matter? Where are you all off to?'

No one answered. Shutters were being closed, doors bolted, gates slammed shut. The street emptied and soon only a chicken was left picking in the dust in the middle of the road. 'Chick, chick, chick,' Leonard clucked, and again, louder: 'Chick, chick, chick.' But the chicken paid no attention and continued impassively to ply its dusty trade. It wasn't frightened, it didn't run away, but neither did it respond to his summons. And as he watched the chicken, the Generalissimo realised that the earth was shaking. He put his ear to the ground and heard a distant, only just audible, metallic vibration.

Not a soul did he meet all the way back to the H.Q. The recent violence, he now realised, had been confined to a few streets, but all the towns-folk—perhaps frightened by the distant rumbling which was growing louder—had crept into their lairs and were sitting tight.

A hundred yards away from his house, Leonard heard the bells shrilling in his study; he sprinted the rest of the way. The front door stood wide open and the wind was blowing through the rooms. The gashes in the wallpaper gaped. But science hadn't let him down: the signalling system worked normally. Lights were flashing on and off on his desk, encircling the plan of the city. The circle was narrowing. Makepeace tried to scrape a hundred-rouble note off the wall with his penknife, but the blade slipped. Now there were no more flashes or bells: all the cables had been cut.

'Vitya! Vitya!' shouted Makepeace as he wheeled his bicycle into the yard. There was no reply. The workshop was deserted. Leonard could feel the ground quaking under his feet.

'Vitya!' he called once again before putting his weight on the pedals.

The rumbling was ever louder. Amphibious tanks were advancing upon the city from three sides. Like up-to-date brontosaurs, they waddled through the gulleys, sailed across the swamps, crashed their way through woods of stunted fir and weedy birch, and came out plastered with mud and scum and wreathed in water lilies and branches of trees. If they trampled the crops, fences and huts as they came to them, it was not out of spite or for tactical advantage but because they were guided by radio from a great distance away and although their instruments were highly sensitive they couldn't always identify the nature of the obstacle, such as a tree or a house, which stood in their way. Unmanned, empty, they advanced like armour-plated cattle, without shooting, merely crashing through and trampling down the way into the future.

A man with a gun jumped out of a hedge and fired two rounds of small shot at one of the monsters: Vitya Kochetov refused to surrender Lyubimov without a shot. The monster paused as though wondering what to do with such an adversary. It strained all its sound and photo-registering apparatus but registered nothing. After standing for a while in what seemed a reflective silence, it lashed out with a short cautionary broadside at the street. Cut in half, the former agent and only defender of the city fell without a groan.

Chapter Seven
And Last

———————————————————————————

Towards the end of summer there came to Father
Ignatius a pilgrim, a poor old woman, a stranger
from the city—from Lyubimov, she said—and
how a frail old woman had dragged herself over
fifty miles on foot through the forest and survived
the journey was a wonder to everyone. She
brought him a cottage cheese wrapped in a clean
rag, and three roubles in money to pay for two
services: one for the welfare of Leonard, Servant
of God, the other for the soul of the deceased
Servant of God, Samson.

'Recently deceased?' asked the priest who liked
to do things properly and to know what he was
about. 'A fine old name, Samson,' he added
respectfully.

'Ever so old, Father, ever so old,' the old
woman was pleased. 'There's nothing recent
about him at all.'

'Is it true, Mother, can you tell me—they say

there's been a lot of trouble in Lyubimov, sin and law-breaking and sedition and affray, and that some people have suffered for their faith in Christ and for Holy Church?'

'There's been all kinds of trouble, Father, all kinds of trouble'—but as to what exactly had happened in Lyubimov, she seemed unable to say.

Father Ignatius's parish was the poorest imaginable, so tucked away in the wilds that the ancient church might have been standing at the end of the world, clinging to its very edge as it were, and perhaps the reason it was still standing was that it was indeed at the end of the world, where few visitors came and the only people it could comfort were a few old women, so old that they ought long ago to have been dead.

But the priest prayed with fervour, taking his time over the ritual and observing it scrupulously, though he had to do everything himself, as he had no assistants. Somehow there were always a few old women at every service, three or four on weekdays and more on Sundays and feast days. They were there as usual the day the pilgrim arrived, spread over the floor of the church like large, old, worm-eaten forest mushrooms, prostrating themselves and praying for the sins of the fathers and of the sons, of the living and of the dead.

The priest said the liturgy for the living and then for the dead—first for Leonard and then for Samson; he chanted and sang, and burned incense and lit candles, doing it all himself. And although the woman had only given him a cottage cheese and three roubles, he decided to say still another prayer for the dead, although it wasn't in the rubrics. He was very fond of this prayer—it had come to Russia from the Holy Mountain of Athos itself—and he knew that a strong and holy prayer could do no harm either to Samson or to the city beloved of God, which had been through so much that summer.

'Our Father,' he prayed, 'grant joy to the souls of those who were broken by the storms of life. Grant them, our Father, to forget the tears and sorrows of their life on earth. Take them to Thy bosom, our Father, and comfort them as a mother comforts her children.'

Slow, heavy, unwilling to let go, the earth was forced at last to release its hold and the soul ascended, shedding the memory of its earthly sorrows, laughing and trembling at the speed of its ascent and at the shaft upon shaft of light which pierced its clear, airy substance, aware of nothing but the joy of its long awaited release . . .

' . . . save, O Lord, all those who have died in torment, all who were slain, immured, devoured by water or earth or fire, or killed by hunger or cold, or by falling from a height, comfort them for their mortal pain and give them Thy everlasting joy . . . Our Father, give rest to those who were crushed by the burden of their labours. Quench the sorrow of parents who mourn their children. Grant Thy peace, O Lord, to all who have died bereaved, lonely, destitute, or have no one to pray for them . . .'

The priest chanted and called upon God in his sturdy voice. He knew of the evil that had befallen Lyubimov—sin and sedition and persecution and bloodshed—and he wanted his prayers to cover it and obtain from God the salvation of His servants, whatever death they had died and whatever the burdens they had died with. Being only a village priest, he was not a learned theologian, but one thing he knew: that even if his church were the last on earth, he must stay at his post on the edge of the world and continue to work for the salvation of impious men— continue to work like an ox, like a labourer, like a king—like the Lord God Himself whose works are as infinite as His mercy.

'Our Father,' he vociferated with solemnity, 'we grieve at the obduracy of the lawless blasphemers of Thy holy name. Our Father, let Thy saving will be done in them. Have mercy, our Father, on those who are stricken with the mortal sickness of unbelief. Their sins are great but Thy mercy is greater. Our Father, forgive all those who have died unrepentant. Our Father, save those who have killed themselves in the insanity of their despair. Save them, Father, for the sake of the faithful who cry unto Thee night and day. Our Father, forgive the sins of the parents for the sake of their innocent babes, and let the tears of the mothers atone for the sins of their children . . .'

The mothers were there, spread all over the floor of the church like old mushrooms, so old and humped and tottering it was a wonder they were still alive. Where did they find the strength to keep alive, let alone to drag themselves to church? What could possibly be the use of them?

Nothing in his pockets and not a penny to his name, the noose behind him and no known destination ahead—what advice could anyone have given him? Only to slip out of the village at night, go to the station and, prudently keeping away from the platform and the station police, wait for a goods train—and meanwhile to put his hands in his pockets and take a stroll.

Pockets are a wonderful thing! You mightn't think that empty pockets would be much use, but the fact is that you have only to put your hands in your trouser pockets and you immediately feel a little quieter in your heart. Poor as it is, a sort of house has been built, a sort of corner has been found where you can be at home and at peace. The friendly warmth of your leg meets you through the thin, worn lining, and you only wish you could get the whole of yourself into your pocket, and sit rolled up in a ball, drowsily sniffing the mixture of smells—cloth and the innocent and always surprising smell of your own skin and the airy dryness of breadcrumbs.

Stealing along the railway track and glancing warily over your shoulder, you hug a remnant of warmth to your stomach and hide from pursuit in your pocket as in a refuge opening out on a secret, invisible life. Where could you hide deeper, cry more cosily? Who can you share your thoughts with better than with your pocket?

. . . a drink would be nice . . . and a stroll along the platform . . . hands in your pockets . . . cousin to a king . . . Why not? Who cares ? . . . But if they stop you—'Hands up!'—and slip the catch, and turn your pockets inside out . . . No, better not to be a man who walks this earth with his pockets turned inside out.

. . . luckily a goods train braked at the station and whisked him off. Tucked away in the shelter of tall crates on the floor of an open wagon, Lenny lay drowsily spitting and thinking of nothing. Never in his life had he felt so free, so cosy and relaxed. The yoke of responsibility and the torments of love, cares, fears, memories dropped off and were left behind on the track. Lenny knew that he would somehow have to get some money and a passport and clothes and a job—not too near, perhaps in the Donbas or in Chelyabinsk or in Karaganda . . . But his destiny, he was convinced of it, would take over and without the slightest effort on his part present him with someone else's papers, and a corner to live in, and a bicycle repair shop. Once he had that, he would send for Vitya and Vitya would come, and everything would be all right again, better than ever, running as smoothly and effortlessly as on sleepers. The engine whistled softly, soothingly, as only Vitya knew how to whistle with a file or a chisel in his hands, and the train bore Lenny away in its embrace.

Hi, Professor! Why don't I hear from you any more? Why don't you ever come and nag at me as in the old days, and tell me what to write, now that I am getting so near the end? Why don't I see your corrections on my text or your crest on my dingy writing paper? Maybe you think that I also have died and that the city of Lyubimov is completely destroyed and no longer has anything in it worthy of your interest? Things are not as bad as all that, you know, though it's almost a year since we ceased to be an independent kingdom and reverted to our earlier status of regional centre. Some people were picked up, of course, and some have never been heard of again. —You can't make an omelette without breaking eggs. But a number of houses and even whole streets are intact, and others have already been rebuilt and are filled with newcomers. The monastery is still standing. And as you see, I'm alive and kicking, safe and sound, as I hope this finds you. I did have a spot of bother of course—I could hardly expect not to. But Semyon Gavrilovich Tishchenko, God bless him, gave evidence and cleared me of involvement in the events. It is true that he has been demoted to a secondary role (he is no longer First Secretary) but the views of so outstanding a personality are bound still to carry a lot of weight. So you could safely look me up of an evening as you did in the past. Besides, I assure you that I never sit down to write without bolting my door, so you needn't be afraid of people dropping in . . . Seriously, why don't you, Professor? Couldn't you at least give me a sign? Only write one letter somewhere between the lines and I'll understand and believe everything . . . No? You disappoint me, you know. It's not as if I'd ever begrudged you anything. Didn't I write your biography? And look at Lenny's mother who ordered a requiem for you, paid three roubles out of her own pocket—and you can't be bothered with an old colleague who asks you a favour. Look, Samson Samsonovich, it's not for myself I ask, and not for the sake of this book, which I've nearly finished without you. It's our city I worry about, our country, our native country—*your* native country, Mister Proferansov, the country you have turned your back upon and betrayed! All right, all right, I was only joking. Why don't we pool our efforts once again, and have a really good try and give the wheel of history one more turn? All you have to do is give us back our Lenny Makepeace, our Tsar, our will, our—energy—or whatever you call it—and we'll build you communism once again in no time at all . . .

Strictly between ourselves—but you really mustn't breathe a word, Professor—I told you a lie when I said that things were not as bad as they might be. The fact is, they couldn't be worse. The investigation continues. Any moment there will be a new wave of arrests. If they search the house and find this manuscript under the floorboards, they'll pick up every single one of us. Listen to me, Professor. After all, you are my co-author. Will you hide this wretched book away for the time being? Keep it in your inaccessible safe for the present? You took your own book back from Lenny so you must have some locker or safe—any hiding place . . . —Look after it for a bit. You do recognise it as your property, don't you?

DATE DUE